DAPHNE'S WEB

L. L. CARTIN

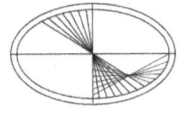

DIVERTIR
PUBLISHING
Salem, NH

I0627801

Daphne's Web

L. L. Cartin

Copyright © 2018 L. L. Cartin

Cover design by Kenneth Tupper

Author photo by Jaime Bley

This is a work of fiction. Any resemblance to actual persons, living or dead, or actual events is purely coincidental.

Published by Divertir Publishing LLC
PO Box 232
North Salem, NH 03073
http://www.divertirpublishing.com/

ISBN-13: 978-1-938888-23-6
ISBN-10: 1-938888-23-5

Library of Congress Control Number: 2018966256

Printed in the United States of America

Acknowledgment

Daphne's Web unfolded from a synchronistic merging of people, places, and events. The storyline began in my Victorian home during a series of metaphysical classes when participants were frequently disrupted by unsettling supernatural activity. I invited two separate teams of paranormal investigators to validate and document the presence of ghosts. I thank both teams as well as the spirits in my house for inspiring this mystical work of fiction.

Thank you to my early manuscript readers who stuck with it to see if the story was a grabber and gave spot-on critiques which helped me stay on track. I especially thank my loving family, who I assume thought I was crazy but kept their opinions to themselves.

As a first time author, I foolishly believed all one needed for a novel was a good story and passion for writing. I gratefully acknowledge the editors of the initial, final, and final-final edits before the final edit leading to other final edits (sigh). Of course, it was Dr. Kenneth Tupper of Divertir Publishing who saw the potential and made it happen.

Follow L. L. Cartin at

http://schoolfordreams.blogspot.com
http://facebook.com/LLCartin

Contents

PROLOGUE 1956

NORMAN PALMOURE INHALED a deep drag from his cigarette and snuffed its remains into the overflowing ashtray on his gray, metal desk. He leaned back on a swivel chair to put his feet up while savoring the moment of having sold the infamous Victorian house belonging to the late Dr. Arthur Wake. It was the final detail in a long, messy estate settlement. The generous commission made the sale all the more sweet. Norman clasped his hands behind his head and contemplated another vacation.

"Hey Doug, come with me to put the sold sign on the Main Street property. I'll buy you a drink to celebrate," he offered his business partner.

"Someone actually bought that nightmare?"

Norman nodded, shrugging his shoulders.

"Right...and I bet you're telling me about the sale now because you already unloaded the antiques and made yourself a bundle." Doug was annoyed, thinking he missed out again.

"Nah, it sold yesterday afternoon to a woman with two kids. She's keeping everything the estate left behind."

"What's she like?" Doug asked. "There's probably more to it since you never let expensive furniture slip through your fingers."

"Honestly, the broad's a bit of an oddball, but she's perfect for that old house."

"Is she a looker?" Doug glanced at his partner, a handsome guy with one glob too many of pomade in his thick, black hair.

"Yeah, one hell of a looker," Norman muttered, outlining an hourglass figure with his hands. "I could sure go for those green eyes and pretty face, but..."

"But what?"

"Her husband is Marc Betel, the big-shot criminal lawyer from the city."

"Oh—I guess with all his money, they'll restore the dump, make it a showplace, and entertain the hoity townsfolk. That'll leave you out," Doug teased.

"Not exactly," Norman corrected, ignoring the sarcasm. "She was obsessed with the place and told me it was calling out to her, whatever that meant. Even wilder, the husband insisted he would never live in it. He wrote me a check right there on the front porch without stepping inside. It was like he couldn't wait to get the hell away."

"Go figure."

"There's more. Get this—Betel bought the house and then wrote her a check for fifty grand to renovate it, but she ripped up his check on the spot."

"The lady probably has money of her own."

"I don't think so. Actually, Betel asked me to keep an eye on her. He said she almost drowned recently, and now he thinks she's going nuts."

"And in that house, going nuts will happen sooner rather than later," Doug snickered.

"Who cares? Betel gave her what she wanted just to keep the peace, and I got what I wanted. That's why the deal was so quick."

"You like being a hero to beautiful damsels in distress, so I'm sure you'll be paying her a few visits like the last gal you sold a house to."

"Over my dead body," Norman mumbled as he stood up to leave the office. He smoothed back his hair, rolled down his shirtsleeves, and reached for his sports jacket, flinging it across one shoulder. Norman mulled over Mrs. Betel's response when he questioned how she could afford to repair the house on her own. To reject fifty thousand dollars was crazy, but not half as crazy as her glib pronouncement, the house will take care of everything.

The phone rang, and Doug gestured for his partner to go without him. Just as Norman opened the door, hail the size of gum balls pelted the ground. He grabbed an umbrella and walked out with a SOLD sign and mallet.

"Gees, Norm, worry about the damn sign later," Doug called after him, holding a hand over the phone's mouthpiece.

The office door slammed shut. Norman was superstitious and feared they could be stuck with that white elephant another three years if he didn't get the sign up. Despite its run-down condition, the turn of the century Victorian was prime waterfront real estate and should have sold easily. Unfortunately, it made a formidable impression on every prospective buyer.

Riding down Main Street, Norman could barely see through the heavy rain and sporadic pounding of hail. He parked his brand new, two-toned '56 convertible with white-walled tires in front of the house to wait for the weather to calm down. Looking across a crumbling cement path leading to a sorry wreck, Norman imagined how elegant the place must have been when built in the 1890s.

Peeling layers hinted at its history of being a Painted Lady. The roof-line was enhanced with ornate, gingerbread gables. On the right side was a soaring tower, a stack of rounded rooms on every floor. It rose above the contoured roof to a pointed turret.

Norman believed town gossip about the original owner going half-mad in the house. Just walking onto the rickety porch and through the massive double front doors was creepy enough for him. One's eyes would instantly be drawn up the sweeping, spiral staircase leading to bedchambers and baths. Norman was glad his clients never asked to go upstairs.

He purposely removed the basement light bulb because something down there felt as though it had been lying in wait for decades. Whatever it was, he didn't want it disturbed—not on his watch. For three years, the house frightened away everyone, except for the undaunted new owner.

When the rain persisted, Norman gave up and decided to return to his office. Just as he shifted into drive, a bolt of lightning struck the Victorian, hitting the metal finial jutting up from the turret. In slow motion, the crackling current traveled down the tower, grounding itself in a sizzling burst of light. The flash illuminated a SOLD sign already on the front lawn.

Norman was spooked. He was the only agent with the listing, so who or what put the sign there? His hair stood up along the back of his neck. He floored the gas pedal and sped off, skidding down the street, swearing he would never set foot on the property again.

CHAPTER 1

Moving Day

"SHH...I'M HERE."

Daphne Betel wheeled around, expecting to find a man standing behind her, but the stifling attic room in her Victorian was empty of everything except cobwebs, a wooden chair, and an old steamer trunk. The wind chime hanging by the back door sounded a hollow ring she heard on the top floor of the rambling house. Feeling a chill, Daphne grasped the collar of her blouse and pulled it closer to her neck.

Since her brush with a watery death two months earlier, Daphne was forced to make many adjustments. All she remembered of the accident was being revived on wet sand and the sweet breath of life filling her burning lungs. Everyone noticed a difference in her personality from then on. Her physician said memories might come back little by little. Daphne was hopeful time would also eliminate an onset of migraines she now dealt with, but was told it might be a painfully slow process. Regardless, moving into the Victorian was something she simply had to do.

"Shh..."

Daphne heard the whispery male voice announcing itself a second time. She wiped beads of sweat from her brow. "My nerves are shot," she exhaled. Spotting a faint outline on the wood-planked floor, she remembered a piece of furniture having been there when the realtor allowed her to roam the upper stories on her own—a handsome, carved mahogany bookcase.

Something shiny was left in its place. Daphne stooped to pick up the striking floral spray, studded with diamonds and attached to a sterling hair clip. Admiring the jeweled piece, she blew off clinging dust and carefully put it into the pocket of her slacks.

The sun cast beams of muted light through the attic's dirty windows, revealing a door previously obscured by the bookcase. Daphne opened it, expecting another dingy room with falling plaster and exposed lath. What she saw astounded her—it was the turret. Narrow windows lined curved walls that towered upward, tapering to its pinnacle. They displayed a 360-degree view of a town nestled into a rocky harbor along the northeastern Atlantic coast. In the center of the floor was an old, claw foot bathtub. She thought it strange the door to this extraordinary room had been concealed.

"Mom," Daphne's ten year old daughter, Nancy, called out. "The movers want to know where to put the big mirror we found in the basement."

"I'd like it up here." Daphne's voice echoed down the long, winding staircase as she made an instant change of plans—the full-length mirror belonged in the turret instead of her bedroom. She leaned over the banister to watch the men awkwardly carrying a walnut-framed, beveled mirror set in a solid stand. The children followed close behind. Once reaching the attic, the men looked ashen and nervous. Daphne's daughters grabbed their mother's hands.

"What's the problem, fellas, was it really that heavy?"

"No, that wasn't it, ma'am," one answered, trying to control his voice from quivering as he hurried down the steps. Daphne wondered why they left the mirror on the attic landing without asking where she wanted it. Their sudden retreat made her anxious. Something was not quite right.

"Mommy, will you come with us while we look around," Nancy pleaded.

"Weren't you girls having fun in the house by yourselves?"

"Those movers scared us when we were in the basement. They said they felt something spooky," Mary explained as her eyebrows arched high.

"Nonsense, they were just reacting to the dirt floor—it gives off a clammy feeling. Eventually, I'll have cement poured over it so you both can roller skate."

Mary and Nancy remained underfoot no matter what their mother said. Daphne brought them to the kitchen where several boxes of essentials were already unpacked. She opened a drawer and pulled out two brand new flashlights, handing one to each girl. They began flicking them on and off.

"What are these for?" Nancy asked, focusing the beam under her chin and making faces to frighten her eight year old sister.

"Take them while you go exploring," Daphne suggested, hoping the flashlights would be an incentive to move about on their own again. She watched them walk through the dining room, shining light on dark oak moldings framing floor and ceiling, as well as doors and windows. The concentrated light exposed spidery cracks running everywhere, connecting spaces caused by missing chunks of plaster. Daphne sighed as the girls disappeared from view.

"Mommy, come here," Nancy called from the round room off the vestibule.

Losing patience with the interruptions, Daphne reluctantly joined them. Nancy was aiming her flashlight into holes in the walls adjacent to bookcases filled with the previous owner's dusty books.

"There's newspaper back there." Nancy stepped aside so her mother could take a look.

"That's the way they used to insulate these old places. The holes will be patched in due time." Daphne's mind went right to her husband's check she impulsively ripped up. It would have been enough to fix everything.

"Mommy, there's something else," Mary said, tugging on dirty rags.

"Girls, stop! Walls were insulated with whatever could be stuffed behind them. Please leave the room exactly as it is for now, even the books," Daphne insisted, thinking giving them flashlights wasn't a great idea after all.

Once the movers left for the day, the telephone installers arrived to wire the Victorian with an extension on each floor. Nancy and Mary kept busy while Daphne spent much of the afternoon unpacking. When she opened her bedroom closet door to hang up clothing, a cold breeze produced an uncomfortable feeling—a sense of sadness—not coming from her own thoughts, but palpable in the room itself.

"Nancy, did you leave any doors open downstairs?" Daphne yelled out.

There was no answer. Daphne became concerned the children went outside, particularly because the waterfront property had an old, decrepit dock. She cried out their names, desperately hoping they would respond. And they did, but with a most unexpected plea.

"Mommy, we're here. Help us get out," she heard coming from somewhere, muffled.

"Nancy, Mary, where are the two of you?"

Something wasn't making sense. Daphne shouted upstairs to the telephone installers, but they hadn't seen her daughters. She remained motionless before the open closet door. Another cold breeze passed by, causing the scalloped-edge shelf liner to lift. Just as she was about to slam the door shut, part of the rear wall burst open and nearly scared her to death. Daphne gasped as both daughters crawled through a tiny door at the back of the dark closet.

"Mommy, we were in a secret hallway behind the walls!" Mary blurted out.

Daphne and the girls plopped down on her bed as she calmed herself enough to ask them how they found the passageway.

"There's another tiny door in the back of my closet. It connects to yours," Nancy eagerly reported.

Daphne explained this was nothing unusual, considering the way houses were built in those days. Regardless, the nooks and crannies now seemed menacing to her. The telephone workers interrupted them. They finished the job and wanted their pay. Daphne insisted the children come with her down the narrow, back staircase to get her purse from the kitchen so the men could leave.

Not long after, the phone rang, and Nancy hurried to answer it. "Daddy, hi. Yes…uh…everything's good…I think. Mommy, come here. Daddy wants to speak to you."

Daphne waited for her daughter's conversation to finish. She became increasingly nervous with every passing second as her mood was changing. Nancy turned the phone over to her mother.

"What do you want, Marc? No…we're fine. No…there's nothing we need, but thanks for asking." Hearing her husband's voice stirred many strong emotions. She cut the conversation short so he wouldn't cause her to cry. The phone rang again. "Hello? Hello?" Daphne raised her voice, agitated. "Marc, is this you? Say something," she demanded, and hung up when there was only dead silence on the line.

A headache flared, reminding her she had to slow down and put one foot in front of the other if living without a husband was going to work. Daphne thought back to all the years Marc kept her under his thumb, insisting he know where she was and who she was with. This was her chance to be on her own, but in the moment, having him around might have made the house feel less frightening.

"Shh…I'm here."

"That voice! That voice!" Daphne put her hands over her ears to block it. She shuddered and turned her back to her daughters to avoid further frightening them, but they both knew something was terribly wrong.

"Mommy, I want to call Daddy," Mary whined, on the verge of tears.

An oppressive atmosphere filled the air. Daphne hadn't noticed anything of the sort prior to purchasing the property. At the time of her decision, she was drawn to the Victorian and its furniture—not paying attention to much else—not even her husband's out-of-character agreement to let her move there without him.

§§§

By evening, the girls fell asleep, and a blanket of quiet descended upon the house. Hoping to find relief from the day's upsetting events, Daphne climbed the stairs to take a bath in the turret's claw foot tub—the thought of which stayed with her since morning. To brighten the space, she lit several candles and dragged the mirror to stand near the tub. A sweet, lavender-vanilla aroma permeated the air as bath salts were poured under hot, running water.

While the tub was filling, Daphne walked to the old steamer trunk under an eave. She loosened the buckles on its worn, leather straps and raised the lid. It felt like it was being pushed back down—then closed with a thud, almost catching her fingers. Steam began spreading throughout the vacant attic space, surrounding the trunk. Daphne hurried to the turret room, thinking the lid was just too heavy.

At last, the tub was full and Daphne readied herself for a long, luxurious soak. She undressed before the mirror, letting the robe slide off her shoulders and drape around her ankles. While pinning up her chestnut brown hair with the diamond clip found earlier, a sinking feeling tightened her stomach. Daphne could have sworn another hand slipped over hers.

She looked into the mirror again. Someone else's dark, searing eyes appeared to be looking back. She panicked and jumped away, hitting something by the tub with her foot. It was a small, rectangular brass placard that read Doctor Is In. The message on it was unnerving, as though the former owner was also in the room. She wrapped a towel around her naked body and put the little sign face down on the attic floor outside the turret door.

The fragrance in the air calmed her unsettling thoughts. A determined Daphne stepped into the bath. She rested her head back and closed her eyes, falling into a light sleep, but then abruptly sat forward—alarmed. Silky strands brushed along her arm. Although assuming they were a lingering cobweb, Daphne still couldn't shake off the sense someone actually was in the room. Remembering all the doors had been locked after the workers left, she felt reassured.

The warm water soothed her back into a light sleep, but she was disturbed again. She swatted the air, thinking it was a persistent spider. There was another brush and another—this time across her face. Daphne was defenseless against the attic bugs or whatever remained unseen in the mist. The sound of footsteps circled the tub. Her mind raced, fearing the realtor might still have a key. Without her knowing, he could have let himself in to hide anywhere in the huge house.

"Who's here?" Daphne yelled out.

She kept perfectly still, barely breathing. Something gently dipped into the water and it rippled—as if stirred by a finger. Daphne tried screaming. Her throat was paralyzed and no sound came out. She held her hands on the water's surface to stop the movement, but it intensified, splashing water about, dousing most of the candles. The turret got much, much darker.

A cold, tingly kiss pressed against her lips. She grabbed the rim of the tub as the room whirled. The water heaved. Her words were finally set free. "No...no!"

"Shh...I'm here."

CHAPTER 2

The Collapse of 13 Years—From Woe to Woo

DAPHNE'S FRIGHTENING FIRST evening turned her reality upside down. Initially, she wondered if it was a dream brought on by exhaustion, but in truth, Daphne knew she faced a very real situation with no escape. She came to grips with a preposterous fact—a strong, masculine spirit was also dwelling in her house.

In the weeks that followed, she tried staying upbeat, going about the chore of organizing her possessions, ignoring the feeling she was being watched. Each time she opened the closet door in her bedroom, that disconcerting breeze lifted the shelf liner ever so slightly.

Her apprehension spiked the day she experienced a cold puff of air directly on the back of her neck. Daphne could actually hear a breath. There could be no mistake—she wasn't alone. It was hard to accept she was stuck with an entity capable of foisting himself upon her world of substance—and against her wishes. With no money to move again, and not wanting to subject herself to Marc's ridicule, this was her home, like it or not.

The ghost's small encroachments became brazen. Daphne began hearing rumbling words she didn't understand and was petrified when hands she couldn't see grabbed her shoulders to immobilize her. This incited greater trepidation each time.

Marc, trying to gain favor, presented Daphne with flowers on his weekend to pick up the children. She put the bouquet in her cherished crystal vase he gave her as an anniversary present and placed it upon a marble table in the vestibule. If Daphne gave Marc's attempts at reconciliation serious thought, she would have begun to connect ghostly activities with her husband's expressions of interest.

Alone in the house, she heard loud tapping coming from the attic. Determined to stop these otherworldly intrusions, she boldly climbed the staircase. The aged wooden steps creaked and groaned. The higher she went, the more the stairs changed—less worn from use, narrower, darker.

Daphne tried turning on an electrified oil lamp along the wall, but it didn't work. Fiddling with the switch, she was momentarily distracted. When she looked up, a dark shadow in human form reached down to grab her. Crying out, she nearly fell backwards before being whisked to the attic in one swoop.

"Don't touch me, get away!" she screamed, aggressively punching her fists into the air. Her breath formed a frosty vapor.

The hair on her arms stood at attention with the onset of an odd noise. Daphne trembled as she turned her head in the direction of a grating sound. Moving on its own, the trunk scraped across the floor planks, its leather straps dragged behind, leaving tracks in the dust. She wanted to run from the attic, but remarkably—the urge subsided.

Daphne lifted the trunk's lid with surprising ease and removed a cloth-wrapped bundle lying on top. She sat on the chair nearby to untie a ribbon holding it together. There was a stack of old, copper molds for making chocolate. Underneath the molds was a worn, leather notebook which had Fixings inscribed on the cover. She read aloud the dedication inside—To Olivia.

Daphne felt a headache coming on. The notebook fell off her lap, jolting her. She picked the book up and thumbed through it. One page was dog-eared to a hand written recipe for, of all things, chocolate. Bemused, she turned more pages. Each one had a special fixing to delight a refined woman of the day—complexion crèmes, hair treatments, herbal teas, and therapies to ease aching bones and calm restless minds. Her headache seemed to lessen. Unconsciously, Daphne passed her hand over her cheek, checking whether her skin felt smooth to the touch.

Daphne examined the rest of the trunk's contents. She lifted sewing tools and fabrics and peeked at what was lying at the bottom, but abruptly dropped it all back into place. The lid slammed shut on its own. Only the copper molds and notebook returned with her to the kitchen. The house seemed more peaceful, as though the entity was satisfied, if not gone.

§ § §

By evening, Daphne readied for bed, dressing in warm pajamas. The late autumn air was nippy, and she looked forward to a restful night at last, falling into a deep sleep under a soft comforter. But to Daphne's horror, she was awakened by a crushing pressure on her body. An invisible weight held her captive. Slow, deliberate breathing could be felt against her face. Trying to pull away, she broke into a pouring sweat.

"You're mine."

No other words were spoken. The pressure lifted and the breathing was gone. Terrified, Daphne's eyes searched the dark room. All was as it should be. She stretched one arm to switch on the lamp by her bed to check the time. It was 3 AM. Descending to her lowest ebb, Daphne curled on her side, pulled up her knees, and wept until the sun rose.

Exhausted, she stayed in bed the next morning. Nancy and Mary were still with their father and would not return until evening, giving her time to nurse another severe migraine. It seemed the doctor had been waiting for exactly this moment. A deep indentation formed in the mattress where he sat. Daphne's heart beat faster, and the headache became blinding.

"Please, please, let me be…don't hurt me."

"Shh…"

A soft, loving stroke of a misty hand soothed her. His touch was magical—healing. Daphne's migraine disappeared in an instant. All her misgivings miraculously ceased. She realized the spirit meant her and her daughters no harm, but now she had a nagging thought—what did he want?

§ § §

Over time, Daphne became more relaxed with the ghost and often awaited his arrival. When he didn't appear, she grew restless, like a scorned lover. Unable to erase him from her thoughts, she tried out different ways to draw him to her.

Late one night, when the house was quiet and the children asleep, Daphne felt inspired to prepare a batch of chocolate. Entering the kitchen, she lit several candles, pulled out the stack of copper molds, and studied the recipe in the notebook. From the corner of her eye, she witnessed one tray slowly slide across the counter toward the mixing bowl, leaving behind a trace of ghostly light. Taking a minute to collect herself, she noticed each hollow in the tray had the same embossed image, a circle, and wondered its significance to her spectral resident. She soon learned he would manifest whenever she made chocolate.

The ghost also knew how to woo her and became clever at doing so. The old, grandfather clock in the vestibule struck three times in the wee hours one morning. Daphne heard soft dance music coming from the parlor.

13

Her antique phonograph was cranked up and playing a slow waltz. Feeling like a spectral being herself, she floated down the staircase with bare feet and a longing smile. A delicately stitched, white silk nightgown hugged her curvaceous body and flowed to the floor like a gossamer cloud.

The ever-so-slightly visible, tall, and handsome Dr. Arthur Wake was waiting on the settee, finely dressed in a long-tailed Victorian coat, ascot, and tweed trousers. When he stood up, Daphne stepped into his field of energy. She tingled from head to toe, and the chill of him gave her goose bumps. Arthur was able to transmit a gentle sense of his touch to her hips and extended hand as she positioned herself in a dance pose. Daphne felt an exhilaration that could only be had when the thin membrane of their separate worlds came in contact.

They twirled about the parlor, savoring every fleeting moment he could remain in the earthly realm before being transported back into his dimension. This was the first of many surprise encounters, and whenever he left, Daphne would sulk for hours, anticipating their next rendezvous. As these interludes continued, they set a backdrop for the years that followed, creating a whole new secret life Daphne could reveal to no one. She had fallen head over heels in love—with a ghost.

§ § §

Daphne's change in behavior was noticed by her husband. She seemed happy—almost like her old self before the near drowning. Thinking she had a lover, Marc became jealous and spied on the house. Seeing nothing to make him suspicious, he hired detectives to follow her. No activity out of the ordinary was uncovered.

Desperate, Marc sent letters. They were reported to have disappeared before the mailman's eyes as he attempted to put them into the door slot. Marc's official-looking documents met with the same dead-end. His attempts at phone contact were equally exasperating. Each time Daphne answered, earsplitting static caused her to hang up.

Making a visit in person was even worse for Marc Betel. He would arrive wearing a well-fitted three-piece suit, expensive shoes, and designer sunglasses hanging from the corner of his mouth. His invincible reputation would be damaged before an audience of nosey neighbors when something invariably obstructed him from stepping into the house.

On more than one occasion, he found the battery in his exotic sports car drained and the vehicle needing to be towed. It embarrassed Marc the most when he spotted Daphne witnessing these spectacles from her parlor window. Upon her eyes meeting his courtroom stare, the drapery would close by what he assumed was his wife's doing. Eventually, his efforts were less frequent. Not even the famed criminal lawyer could upset the Victorian's finely-tuned state of affairs.

Once Daphne's husband was successfully out of the picture, Arthur's visitations became more than just romantic. He telepathically infused his dear one with knowledge about the proper use of essential oils and other natural ingredients, taking instructions from the leather notebook. She learned the art of making old-fashioned beauty and health remedies, lost to present-day manufacturing. Through his mentorship, Daphne began generating income by selling the products in exclusive stores. While earnings sky-rocketed, her phantom suitor insisted she keep the details to herself.

This new-found wealth became a blessing for Daphne. During those years, the roof was replaced, copper gutters installed, rotted siding repaired, and lush landscaping put in place around a new swimming pool. This kept the neighbors' interest piqued, and all eyes and ears focused on the Victorian.

It was a mystery where the money was coming from. Daphne's curious rejection of her husband's offer remained the subject of many conversations, thanks to Norman Palmoure's love of gossip. People tried to pry—Marc most of all. However, the overly-possessive ghost shielded Daphne from their interference. She belonged to him now, and nothing would come between them—nothing—including her husband or any other man who might happen along. He would see to it.

§ § §

Throughout the years, both of Daphne's daughters fared well. They were blissfully unaware of the ghost's presence and machinations. Nancy graduated high school and left home to study fashion design in Europe. Two years later, Mary followed her abroad to pursue a musical career as a concert pianist.

Their departure took a toll on Daphne's state of mind. There was no way of describing the deep loss she felt. Her fear of the sea made it impossible to visit the young women by either ship or plane. A sense of melancholy began to dampen her otherwise happy spirit—but this was something for which the doctor already had a remedy.

For well over a decade, Daphne was given devotion, protection, and a means to prosperity by her spectral resident. It was time to collect on his efforts by opening the Victorian to more players in his elaborate scheme, but first, he would introduce his dear one to another level of knowledge.

The Victorian's library still contained the doctor's books, filled with great wisdom from across the ages. Daphne studied night after night, being promised a way to give to others through teaching. Waiting for the ghost to join her, she'd sit in the library on the soft cushion covering a curved bench along its wall. An outline of shimmering lights would appear. When fully visible, he drifted over to an area in his collection. A single book would tip to catch her attention. Daphne took it from the shelf and sat down, allowing the ghost to turn the pages. Ethereal light formed around selected passages which lifted and projected across the wall, leaving behind powerful messages.

Daphne was given no choice about the matter. She became a vessel for vast amounts of arcane knowledge and was inspired to create a school in the house. Dr. Arthur Wake's plan was in place, and various students were to be lured in, until all the right ones came along.

§ § §

It was a blustery winter day, and as Daphne went about her morning chores, something troubled her—Arthur hadn't visited in weeks. None of her feminine wiles or chocolate making was working. In the past, she simply felt his energy without him materializing in one form or another, but now—just stillness. Daphne never had a thought such as this during all the years in her Victorian—Arthur was done with her.

The hours passed, and Daphne felt agitated by the possibility the Invisible world to which she had given so much attention no longer was relevant without the ghost. Agitation turned to anger over wasted years isolated in the old house just to be at the beck and call of a spirit. Tired of being alone, she craved a normal day around real people. On a whim, Daphne decided to get her hair done, an unlikely thing to do without an appointment. She walked into a nearby beauty parlor and was told someone just canceled due to weather.

The beautician sat Daphne in a chair and draped her with a pink cape. "I've never cut your hair before. How would you like it done?"

"I usually wear it long," Daphne explained. "I'll just have a trim and set."

"Are you going out tonight?" the hairdresser asked, being too friendly for Daphne's comfort.

"No, not tonight," Daphne muttered. For a moment, she amused herself imagining how the hairdresser would react if she even told her the half of it.

"Why, I expected a gorgeous lady like you would be out every night. Hey—now I recognize you. I saw you in the boutique down the street selling your beauty products. I bought some." The hairdresser posed in profile for Daphne to admire her flawless complexion.

A pleasant looking woman, maybe late thirties, was sitting in the adjacent chair. She looked at Daphne through bright, gray eyes. "Excuse me," she said. "I couldn't help overhearing your conversation. My name is Amelia Fulton. I was a chemist in a cosmetic research laboratory, and I've also tried your products. I'm amazed at how well they work. Funny, I knew our paths would cross someday."

Daphne didn't encourage discussion on the subject, still honoring Arthur's wish for her health and beauty formulas to remain a secret. The women chatted about other things until the last blue roller went into Amelia's thick, dark hair. Before being led to the back of the shop to sit under the dryer, Amelia wrote down her phone number on a piece of paper and handed it to Daphne.

Daphne smiled and politely stuffed the paper into her purse, having no inkling as to why she would call Amelia.

§ § §

A shopping bag in one hand and key to the back door in the other, Daphne entered her kitchen to the unmistakable scent of roses. She turned on the lights, wondering how anyone could have been inside while she was gone. Yet curiously, a beautiful bouquet of red roses bound with a translucent pink ribbon was lying on the counter. Delicate light shimmered around it. Daphne knew Arthur was back.

She searched for her favorite crystal vase. Upon returning to the kitchen, the roses vanished before her eyes. Daphne reached out one hand to touch the surface where they had been. Her fingers tingled. The vase slipped from the other hand, breaking into smithereens on the floor. The sound of it shattering was eclipsed by a voice out of nowhere.

"Call Amelia."

§ § §

Soon afterwards, Daphne invited Amelia to her home, the only guest who made it past those massive front doors in thirteen years. She and Daphne became fast friends. But as much as Amelia enjoyed socializing with Daphne, she always knew when it was time to leave—something in the Victorian's atmosphere would change. Only after Daphne opened her school and Amelia signed up for a class was she truly comfortable in the house.

CHAPTER 3

1969

A HEAVY SPRING RAINSTORM drenched Franklin Port. Flooding was a frequent inconvenience, but on that day both the high tide and full moon added to the ominous water levels overflowing onto village streets.

Daphne awoke to a loud backfire near her house. She opened the bedroom's French doors and stepped onto the balcony to look below. An old, beat-up truck was rattling along behind a young woman sloshing through ankle-deep water, struggling with an army duffle bag slung over one shoulder. Her rain slicker's hood was sliding off the thick, honey-colored hair braided down her back.

"Good morning," Daphne felt compelled to call out, but the girl kept walking, never glancing up.

Daphne watched the truck stop next to her. A white-haired, heavyset driver got out and opened the passenger door. Daphne was too groggy to ponder why she had been inclined to catch the stranger's attention and went back to bed after the truck drove away. She figured if they were destined to meet, it would happen—of that she had no doubt.

§ § §

"Hey missy, why are you walking so early in this miserable weather?" Gus asked Cassandra Renney in his thick Swedish accent.

"I'm getting a jump start," she answered, adjusting the garden tools poking through her duffle bag. "You know me, I can't waste any time—I have to get the soil ready for planting. Today is the first day of spring."

Cassandra was a beauty of sturdy stock, modest about her natural endowments, with a work ethic Gus respected. Not only did she hold down a job as a library clerk, but Cassandra was also devoted to gardening. She shifted the bag into a more comfortable position across her lap, explaining how her car was parked several streets away due to the flooding.

They headed up the hill toward the entrance of what was once a prominent estate. Huge, black iron gates had the name Hidden Arbor Cemetery scrolled into the intricate, woven design of trumpet flowers and curling tendrils. Cassandra looked across the seat at the cemetery's caretaker and recalled the first time they met, two years before, after her mother passed away. Gus often said he admired the beautiful flowers she planted at the gravestone and her generosity in giving them to fellow mourners. His friendliness made it easy to talk to him about her unfortunate childhood.

Cassandra's father died when she was eleven, leaving her and her older brother to keep their family farm going. Their mother had few resources and even fewer options to run the farm and feed everyone. Working the soil is in my blood, she told Gus on more than one occasion—the very reason he shared stories with her as well.

The truck chugged into the cemetery. Cassandra stared ahead at a barren dirt road leading to an overgrown thicket. She knew from Gus all the land once belonged to wealthy settlers who created a spectacular arched arbor of blooming flowers drawing many townspeople for their marriage ceremonies. He also claimed an old farmhouse was beyond the arbor. Although everything was now heavily enshrouded under unrestrained brambles, Cassandra was charmed by his story's romantic notion. To the south of the choked thicket was the sun-drenched field Gus offered Cassandra to plant a garden, making her a part of the land's history.

Cassandra jumped at the opportunity Gus presented, even though it was in such a strange location. She wanted to grow vegetables for a local food pantry and one day build a business—a line of canned condiments and delicacies using family recipes.

Cassandra looked again at Gus while the pickup sputtered along the road. As they passed the imposing thicket toward the open field, Gus turned to her and grinned. She smiled back, wondering what he was thinking. The truck stopped and Cassandra got out, thanking her friend for the ride.

She worked tirelessly preparing the land, pulling up old roots and stubborn weeds to ready it for seeding on another day. Cassandra looked over the morning's effort and pictured a harvest more abundant than previous seasons. Her life was going to change—she just knew it.

Before leaving, she placed her tools in the moss-covered stone outbuilding bordering the thicket. As she closed the door to the shed, she remembered a familiar apprehension, catching her off guard. There was no wind, but Cassandra heard spoken words rippling through the air—conversation.

She cringed, dwelling on what remained behind. The weathered head-stones down the road and the light filtering through the trees formed scary shadows. The smell of rich soil made her feel heady, but the sweet, fruity scent of Gus's pipe tobacco drifting past eased her concerns.

Cassandra's attention was again drawn to the gnarled thicket where sun could not penetrate. Although intrigued by the secrets it must hold, she would never dare to venture in by herself. Cassandra brought her thoughts back to that which she could grasp—at least the duffle bag did not have to be lugged to the car.

The weather cleared as she walked out the gates onto puddled roads. Cassandra took time to admire a rainbow forming in the sky over the homes on Main Street. It had brilliance, the likes of which she never saw before. Spanning one house in particular, the scarlet slice of the spectrum of light appeared to be touching a stunning, fully refurbished Painted Lady with a red gabled roof.

She relished the scenario she was conjuring up—owning the grand-est house in the neighborhood, the huge, colorful Victorian directly in front of her. Cassandra imagined herself with a family and a loving hus-band who was handsome and ambitious. Chills ran up and down her spine at the grandiose dream of having it all.

Then, lo and behold, she saw a wooden sign hanging from the porch of the Victorian. Cassandra stepped closer to read it. She made a mental note to someday find out what it was all about.

SCHOOL FOR DREAMS
Come In
Daphne Betel, Proprietor

CHAPTER 4

SCHOOL FOR DREAMS

BOO!"

Startled, Daphne stopped rearranging the porch furniture. She turned around to find Amelia standing behind her. "Oh, it's you," she exclaimed.

"I'm so sorry, my mistake. I should never forget this house rattles you at times," Amelia said, watching Daphne drag the wicker chairs back to where they just were. "You seem a little disoriented. Are you okay?"

"Yes, yes." Daphne was abrupt. "What brings you here?"

"Aren't you expecting me?"

"Expecting you for what?"

"You're starting another summer session today, don't you remember? Isn't it why you're sprucing up the front porch for us to hang out beforehand?"

"I'm cleaning, that's all. The class must have slipped my mind. Amelia, do you think I look overweight?" Daphne asked out of the blue.

"Weight was never an issue for you before. Why do you care now? Have you been seeing your husband again after all this time and he's complaining?"

Daphne began wiping down the furniture, ignoring Amelia.

"I've never seen you so unfocused. It must be your husband. You've told me he always wanted you looking perfect. That's what you get for marrying a man with champagne taste."

"Any issues with my husband were long ago. Marc is actually in Europe as we speak, visiting the girls—indefinitely."

"Are you okay with that?" Amelia saw how sad her friend was at the mere mention of her daughters. She changed the subject and pitched in to get the porch ready. "Who's signed up for today?"

"I'm trying to remember. I think Gwen Davens is coming, and a few new women. But you know how things work around here—they come, they go. I'll never understand why."

"Maybe it's your house. It has an overbearing presence at times."

"What do you mean? Never mind, I know what you mean," Daphne agreed. "Look, now I'm rushing. Would you bring out refreshments from the kitchen while I go upstairs?" she asked, hurrying through the front doors.

Amelia filled pitchers with cool drinks to place on the glass-topped tables flanking comfy, wicker chairs. The warm dry air was a welcome relief from steady rains of recent months, and the porch was once again decked out with its multicolored, striped awnings, a magnet for students who gathered early. Amelia greeted a newcomer, Suzanne. Once Gwen arrived, the women settled into soft seat cushions and sipped lemonade, chatting about Daphne's classes.

"Gwen, do you remember your first day in the school and the frantic student who lost her keys?" Amelia asked. "I think you freaked her out when you told her they were lodged in the fireplace grate. I wondered how you could have known. I actually thought you put them there, until Daphne announced something outlandish," Amelia confessed. "Do you recall what she told you?"

Gwen gave a deep laugh, in stark contrast to her slender frame. She swept her coppery red hair off her forehead. Her forte was finding missing things. "Of course I do. It was absurd." Gwen laughed again. "She said with my psychic ability, her ghost might want something from me. But I didn't believe in ghosts and was ready to walk out, like the gal with the keys."

"What made you stay?" Suzanne questioned.

"I couldn't leave. Daphne got up and put her hands on my shoulders."

"No she didn't," Amelia clarified. "Daphne escorted the woman to the door after she called the school a fraud. You know how upset that gets Daphne."

"Oh yeah, I remember, but...but...I actually felt hands on my shoulders holding me in my seat."

"Is this house haunted?" Suzanne asked with a shaky voice. She had been hesitant to register for Daphne's classes because of town rumors about the house and its owner. "Is it?" she repeated when no one answered.

"Maybe," Amelia replied. "The jury is still out. Let's head inside." Amelia got up to lead the way.

The golden oak table in the dining room was always piled high with Daphne's books on one end. Note pads, pens, goblets, and lace glass pitchers of water crowded the rest of it. However, Daphne's usual homemade chocolates weren't there. "I think Daphne is distracted," Amelia said quietly.

She retrieved the dish from the refrigerator to place in its customary spot next to the placard, Doctor Is In.

Daphne was nowhere in sight, giving the three students time to make more small talk. Suzanne studied the room. A sizeable portrait of a woman hung on the wall. Her skin appeared smooth as porcelain, with lips painted fire engine red. Her gently rouged cheeks highlighted green eyes, and her chestnut-brown hair flowed to her shoulders.

"Is that Daphne?" Suzanne asked, pointing to the picture.

"Oh yes," Gwen acknowledged. "It was when she was much younger. It's so odd, Daphne still looks exactly the same," she commented. "Where is Daphne, anyway?"

"She went upstairs a while ago," Amelia replied. "Maybe I should begin the class for her?"

"Yes, please begin so I can get out of here," Suzanne insisted.

Amelia passed around Daphne's chocolates for everyone to select a piece. Suzanne was struck to see Amelia and Gwen close their eyes a moment before putting the chocolate into their mouths, as if there was a purpose to it.

"What were we supposed to do besides eat it?" Suzanne questioned, swallowing.

Amelia smiled. "There's a method to the madness. Each chocolate has a different image. Which one did you choose?"

"I don't know—I didn't look."

"Well, that's the first lesson. We must make ourselves aware of not only what we're doing and thinking, but what's around us."

"Why didn't you tell me before you offered it?" Suzanne asked snidely.

"It's more effective when we learn on our own by being curious, like you are now." Amelia picked up the dish of chocolates and showed her the various raised images. "Each one has its own meaning, similar to common dream symbols. We use these to help focus on our desire. Once we know what we want, we can set an intention. This is the beginning of making dreams come true."

"That can't work. It's too simple," Suzanne argued.

"It's what follows that counts. Daphne's school teaches us the power of our thoughts and how to use them for our benefit. Why not begin with symbols on chocolate?"

They were distracted by a crinkling sound coming down the stairs. "What's that noise?" Suzanne nervously peered through the doorway.

Daphne was making a grand entrance wearing shiny-black plastic garbage bags, cinched together at the waist with a stretchy red belt.

"What kind of outfit is that?" Amelia laughed in disbelief as she turned on the bright lights of the chandelier so they could see it better.

Daphne cast a playful look at the group and responded, "And under this, I'm wearing only transparent plastic wrap."

"I hope we're not supposed to wrap ourselves too," Amelia asserted.

Suzanne looked fidgety, as if ready to bolt from the room. Fishing through her purse for something, she dumped its contents onto the table. "I can't find my keys!" she shrilled.

Gwen approached the fireplace, pulled the keys from the grate, and slid them across the table's surface to the stupefied new student. Smiling at Suzanne, Daphne sat down and introduced herself. As Daphne examined the dish of chocolates, Suzanne leaned forward to see which one Daphne would choose. As usual, she picked the circle.

"Wishing is never enough to make your dreams come true," Daphne began. "You must think differently in order to change what you do. Is anyone here willing to give up old habits for her dream?" she challenged.

"What do you mean?" Suzanne asked.

"If we think the same thoughts, we repeat the same behavior. Then when nothing new happens, our wish fizzles out." Daphne watched Suzanne holding her keys tightly in one hand and patting her outdated bouffant hairdo with the other. "Frankly, you're not going to get a ticket to your dreams here, but you will get the guidance necessary to make dreams come true. It's all up to you. Look at what I'm wearing. Can you even begin to imagine why?" Daphne asked them.

No one could.

"I want to lose weight, and this will help sweat off some pounds," she told them.

"That's silly," Suzanne blustered.

"Sometimes we need to take steps beyond the ordinary, even if others think it's silly. I wore this yesterday, forgetting the electrician was coming to fix the porch light. When I went outside, there I was, looking like what the tide washed up. There he was, standing with a smirk on his face, commenting."

"What did he say?" Amelia prodded.

"Now there's one garbage bag I wouldn't mind taking out," Daphne repeated, amused.

"What did you say?" Amelia asked, dreading being in such a ludicrous predicament.

"I calmly said hello and showed him the broken light. And as you can see by what I'm wearing today, I didn't let myself backslide and give up because of the awkward experience. Not to mention, the light is now fixed."

"I would die, just die!" Amelia wailed.

"Why?"

"I wouldn't want anyone seeing me dressed like that, but if it works, it works. So, are you losing any weight?"

"I'll show you." Casting another one of her looks, Daphne unfastened the belt to remove the upper garbage bag.

"Spare us, we believe you!" Amelia begged.

She and Gwen laughed over the not unexpected zaniness of their teacher while Suzanne maintained a dour look. Daphne stopped dead in her tracks—the chandelier turned off spontaneously and began to twist back and forth. Gwen let out a gasp as a stranger appeared in the doorway.

"Is this the School for Dreams?" Cassandra asked in a shy, little girl voice.

Suzanne had enough, packed up her books, and walked out in a huff. Daphne escorted her to the door. "Next," she said, returning to the group. She invited the bewildered young woman to take Suzanne's seat.

§ § §

Cassandra looked around and admired the elegant, fringed rug and marble fireplace anchoring the room. From where she was sitting, she could see glimpses of the winding staircase and lavish velvet drapery in the parlor. Cassandra glanced out the window at a lovely restored, turn-of-the-century guesthouse, surrounded by mature greenery with a speck of the harbor in the background.

Daphne's carpenter, Jason Wells, entered the room with an inane excuse for being there after seeing a pretty girl walk through the Victorian's front doors. Cassandra locked eyes with him.

Jason was a six-foot tall, muscular man with sandy colored hair and soulful, brown eyes. He was handsome in a way that turned female heads. His broad smile in response to Cassandra's riveting stare sent a shockwave through her. For sure, this was going to be her school for dreams.

Observing it all, Daphne laughed softly to herself once Jason left.

She then passed the chocolate dish to Cassandra who unconsciously took a moon symbol.

By the end of class, only Amelia remained to help straighten the porch and rearrange the table. "Daphne, what's up with you?"

"What do you mean?"

"That getup you're wearing, saying you're trying to lose weight. What's going on?"

"I am trying to lose weight."

"Since when?"

Daphne was quiet and went back upstairs, telling Amelia to stay put. She returned a few minutes later. Draped across her arms was a cerulean blue satin dress, trimmed with hand-made lace. "Isn't it beautiful?"

"Why yes, it's stunning. It looks very old, yet in perfect condition. Where did it come from? Or…should I be asking who gave this to you?" Amelia winked, thinking her friend could use a healthy male relationship.

Daphne twirled around, holding the gown as though it was a dance partner. Without warning, she stopped. "Arthur gave it to me," she whispered. "He left it lying on my bed yesterday morning. But it doesn't fit me yet. I have to lose weight for him."

"Who's Arthur?"

"Dr. Arthur Wake—he's the ghost in the house."

"Cut it out, Daphne. It's bad enough you have me thinking about mystical things, but ghosts giving a dress…come on," Amelia protested.

"You saw for yourself…just before…you saw evidence of Arthur in action."

"Evidence?"

"The chandelier…he turned it off and moved it. He can do things. I thought he was trying to keep me from exposing myself, but then I realized it was something else. It has it do with the new girl, Cassandra."

"You're making no sense. Are you getting one of those migraines you used to have? Here, let me help you upstairs and into bed. I'd stay longer, but Thad will be home from work, and I haven't shopped for dinner yet. You know how grouchy he gets when hungry. I promise to call later."

Amelia exited the Victorian, happy that class was done with.

Wednesday, June 25
Who is this new girl, and what's cooking with her and Jason? ~D~

CHAPTER 5

Frozen in Time

"MAY I HAVE your name, Miss?" the attendant asked, blocking the flashy white coupe from further entering the Victorian's driveway.

"Jacquelyn Daye."

The man scanned the clipboard in his hand. "Are you a student of the School for Dreams?" he asked, not finding her name on the list.

"No," she curtly answered.

"I'm sorry…this party is for past and present students only. I have strict orders not to let in gawkers."

"Idiot, get out of my way. I've been invited by the owner of the house." Jacquelyn rolled her car forward, forcing the man to jump aside. "Lackey," she mumbled to herself, passing him. To the rear of the property was a valet, prepared to park her new vehicle.

"Keep it close by," she insisted, sliding off the red leather seat. "I don't intend to be here long."

The valet sized her up. It was hard not to notice her stunning good looks and sharp tongue. He smirked as she stood there not knowing where to go, and pointed to the gardens where Daphne's Fourth of July party was being held. "Is this your first time?" he asked, getting into the driver's seat.

"First time for what?" she rudely responded.

"Oh…it is your first time." He heartily laughed as he drove her car to the parking area.

Jacquelyn walked toward a huge, white canvas tent erected alongside a swimming pool. The tent was decorated with red and blue helium balloons. Centerpieces of exquisite flowers were on the tables, giving off fragrances holding their own against aromas of fresh food cooking on grills. Women wore floppy brimmed hats and flowery sundresses, adding color to the décor. Jacquelyn self-consciously adjusted the scanty red and blue wrap covering the lower part of her strapless white bikini. She could barely tolerate looking out of place in any social setting.

"What kind of freaky event is this? I thought it was a pool party," she complained out loud to no one in particular.

"First time?" Amelia asked from behind.

Jacquelyn spun around. "Why the hell is everyone asking me the same thing?"

Amelia introduced herself and escorted Jacquelyn to the pool. Some people were sitting on the edge dangling their feet in the water, while others were standing in it up to their necks, as though the water held the magic of Lourdes.

There was an empty Adirondack chair next to where Amelia sat down. "Is this seat taken?" Jacquelyn asked.

"Around here, you can't tell." Amelia laughed loudly, patting it.

Jacquelyn rolled her eyes with annoyance and settled in.

"It won't be much longer," Amelia stated.

"Much longer for what?"

"You'll see." Amelia quietly studied Jacquelyn, guessing she was probably in her twenties. Her long, platinum blonde hair was pulled back in a ponytail, as if hair was so easy for her. Instinctively, Amelia gently flattened her unruly mane into place. She wondered why this girl was invited, aware she'd never been a student at the school. Daphne's annual Fourth of July party was something not publicized around town, as the bewildering incident, which always took place on this holiday, might flame negative stories about the Victorian.

"Jacquelyn, how do you know Daphne?" Amelia was curious.

"I heard her give a library talk. To me, everything she said was nonsense. I don't believe in waving magic wands and saying abracadabra to get results. I'm a scientist—I work in toxicology," Jacquelyn proudly stated.

Amelia, having also been in science, had this defensive conversation before with others. She gave Jacquelyn another once over, knowing it wasn't the right time to drive home the principle that thoughts and words are magic wands. Amelia was certain the party would shake up Jacquelyn's ordered world, as it had done to hers. She could hardly wait for the phenomenon to happen.

Daphne whisked by the chatting women. "Oh, I'm glad you two met," she spoke in passing, tipping her head a bit to glance at them with one of her mischievous looks.

Amelia nodded back. As she and Jacquelyn became more relaxed, a loud shout was heard from the dock. Amelia checked her watch—it was

4:50. The commotion was underway at exactly the same time as in previous years, a reliable attraction captivating Daphne's most psychically sensitive students, particularly Gwen, and terrifying less psychic ones.

Like a moth to a flame, Jacquelyn disappeared into the crowd by the dock, exposing her long lean legs under the beach wrap as she ran. Amelia repositioned herself on the lawn, expecting a particular scene from another realm to play out in the identical spot. This year, Amelia was determined to interact with the main figure in the episode, just to satisfy her mounting curiosity about the Victorian's ghostly activities.

A portion of the baby-blue sky on the horizon turned a deep indigo. The water surrounding the dock roiled, lapping against wooden pilings and splashing over the pier. A rip in the Universe formed, and a muted gray schooner sailed across, creating a sense of alarm for the onlookers. It came forward rapidly—skimming the inky water's surface and traveling through all the pleasure craft, fishing boats, and water skiers who had no awareness of its presence. The horrified guests watched the unfolding scene, as the sailboat headed straight toward the house.

"Why is that boat coming here?" Jacquelyn shrieked with a voice louder than the others.

Amelia noticed Gwen blinking her eyes. When she began rubbing them, Amelia knew Gwen's vision was shifting into sepia tones she once described as having the quality of a turn-of-the-century photograph—like a picture one would find tucked away in an old attic. Gwen abruptly turned her back to the dock and looked up at the turret. Amelia followed with her own eyes, but saw nothing out of the ordinary.

Jacquelyn ran across the yard with the others who were trying to get into the Victorian for protection. Daphne blocked the frantic guests and directed them to either side of the lawn. The crowd waited. Many wanted to leave, but were transfixed, as if under a spell. They heard sails lowering on riggings and the start of engines as the vessel prepared to dock. A brown haze hung over the large craft. It began oozing onto Daphne's property toward the back door, laying an obvious path.

Gwen witnessed something even more upsetting by the dock. "Help! A boy just fell into the water! I can't swim to save him from being hit by the boat! Please help...somebody!"

A few brave souls converged on the platform and searched the water for the child, but he was nowhere to be seen. Jacquelyn laughed out loud, yelling it was all play acting with very believable props. Amelia stiffened at Jacquelyn's dismissive attitude, knowing some implausible situation was desperately trying to reveal itself year after year.

In a split second, a wind pushed the people back, and Jacquelyn became silent. Guests struggled to regain their balance and steady glasses and plates in hand. A wider aisle formed from the disturbance. The water bulged and a green, aqueous mass emerged out of it. One could almost discern the outline of a child in midair, dripping across the path to the back door. On its own, the door opened and then slammed shut, swallowing the watery figure.

An apparition of the boat's skipper, dressed in white nautical clothing, descended the stately vessel's plank. It moved toward the house. Amelia was waiting for this moment and stood directly in his way to block him, but he walked right through her. The breathless crowd gasped. Amelia shivered from the deathly cold under the July sun's heat.

The apparition furiously pounded on the door with both fists and shouted, "This has to stop—he's all that's left!"

The wind chime rang turbulently, and from inside the Victorian came an angry response, "Go away!"

The ghostly skipper turned around, clutching his chest over his heart with both hands. He became less visible with each step he took. His faint figure returned to the boat, whereupon he boarded. The shadowy crew readied the vessel, and it sailed out of the harbor, escorted by a flock of black gulls. The schooner disappeared across the rip in the Universe, which closed up after it. Everything reverted to normal. The whole thing happened so fast, guests, as always, were in disbelief. If asked about it, Daphne would shrug her shoulders and say the past is frozen in time.

Amelia looked at her watch again—still 4:50. She rushed over to Gwen. "Does this make more sense to you yet?"

"No, except a child falling into the water is new information. It must be connected somehow."

Amelia pursed her lips, struggling to understand the meaning behind bits and pieces of the spectral event. "Why were you looking at the turret?"

"I saw a man up there, watching us. He vanished the second the child fell off the dock. Unfortunately, I still can't figure it out. I'm sorry, Amelia."

"I guess we'll be meeting here same time next year," Amelia said, furrowing her brow as she thought it over.

As always, guests whispered to each other about the madness. Some were so overwhelmed by the interruption of reality they remained dazed, while a few sat on the grass, unable to stand for several minutes. It took a while for everyone to get their bearings and return to enjoying the extravagant party. Amelia observed Jacquelyn sunbathing by the pool, as if nothing out of the ordinary happened. "Now, that's a state of denial if I ever saw one," she clucked.

§ § §

The sun was setting below the horizon. A parade began on Main Street ending at Daphne's grand Victorian. A brass quintet, dressed in military uniforms, gathered with other townspeople by the American flag erected on her lawn. Fireworks in the harbor rocketed into the night air, bursting with color and sparkling luminosities in concert with the band's ceremonial performance of the Star Spangled Banner.

A woman's glorious voice, easily reaching the highest notes, rose above other singers in the crowd, punctuating the entire celebration. Amelia looked around and saw it was Jacquelyn singing her heart out in front of the band.

§ § §

Daphne peeked through the kitchen window at her deserted yard. Nothing was left of the party. She put away the last of the dishes and turned off the light.

"Daphne," she heard plaintively spoken in the darkened room. It was a voice seemingly all around. The air chilled and became thick. Arthur was about, but did not materialize, although he was imparting his emotions to her. His world seemed bleak and joyless.

"Arthur, where are you?" Daphne waited, and then felt a weak static charge next to her. She saw an outline hunched over with its head bent low. "Arthur, tell me what's wrong. You remain so distant during these times. I wish you would tell me what the schooner means to you. How can I help if I don't understand?"

She felt the air being sucked out of the room. He was gone.

Friday, July 4th
Sadness remains imprisoned in this house. ~D~

CHAPTER 6

Secrets in the Turret

C LASSES WERE SCHEDULED throughout the summer despite languid afternoons where even a single breeze off the harbor was noticeably missing. The heat was so intense one could fry the proverbial egg on the pavement. Only a few daring students arrived for the first class after the holiday gala—Amelia, Gwen, and Cassandra.

Daphne was nowhere to be seen. A note, written on parchment, was affixed to the fireplace indicating class would be held in the turret, a place where no student ever went before. The three agreed it must be sweltering at the peak of the tower, but worse, they were instructed to find their way alone—one at a time. Standing in the vestibule, they looked up the gloomy stairs to wallpapered corridors with closed oak doors, offering no daylight. Only old, electrified kerosene lamps lit the way. They remembered even Daphne, at times, admitted to getting disoriented in her own house. Their imaginations ran wild with frightening thoughts of encountering the ghost.

"Why can't we go as a group?" Cassandra pressed.

"That's not what we're supposed to do," Amelia reminded her.

They returned to the dining room where there was an odd state of affairs. The table was brimming with a pile of silver goblets and assorted dinnerware. The aberrant heap was in desperate need of polishing.

"Daphne must be expecting us—the chocolate is out. Gwen, you're the official psychic. What's going on here?" Amelia asked, staring at the array of mottled silver.

Gwen took silver polish and rags off the mantle. "Maybe we have some work to do. Daphne has another party coming up. I wouldn't put it past her to expect us to pitch in."

"The note instructed us to go to the turret," Amelia insisted. "What's Daphne thinking with all this silver nonsense?"

"Who knows—but it will keep us busy while we wait our turn."

"I have more important work to do than play games or polish Daphne's silver," Cassandra groaned, thinking about the weeds in her garden.

The wind chime by the back door began to ring wildly. It was not as though a mild breeze had wafted in from the shore, but more as if an impatient schoolmarm called a class to order. Cassandra's arms turned cold.

"Who wants to go first?" Amelia redirected their attention to the note.

Cassandra defiantly rose from the table and stormed into the vestibule. "I will. I want to get this over with."

The sound of her footsteps climbing creaking stairs left a rumbling echo, more exaggerated the higher she went. Cassandra pushed on, overcoming her apprehension, but suspected something did not want her venturing any further. "This is stupid," she spouted.

At that moment, every toilet in the huge Victorian flushed in unison. The old pipes, knocking from the pressure, reverberated throughout the house, sounding like a speeding freight train. It was Cassandra's breaking point. She had enough of Daphne's weird classes and rapidly retraced her steps back down, flying into the dining room. With the color drained from her face, she spewed details of what happened. Amelia and Gwen laughed, but shaken to the core, Cassandra felt she was the butt of a joke. Angry with both of them, she refused their encouragement to try again, picked up her books, and left. The screen door slammed shut.

"Cassandra could use a moon chocolate about now," Gwen teased. "It might help remind her she has a softer side under all that pent-up anger."

Amelia pulled the chocolates closer to study them but could not make out the images. "Look at this—they're melting in front of my eyes. How can I possibly know which one to choose?" she asked, passing the platter to Gwen.

"That's strange. Each one has the same image—a flame. It's as though the symbol itself is melting the chocolate."

"What does a flame mean?"

Gwen paused a moment. "It means transformation. Something old is changing into something new. I think we're in for it today."

"Great." Amelia pursed her lips with anticipation.

Amelia wondered if Cassandra had the right idea and considered leaving as well, when a rare, peaceful calm came over her. She picked up a gooey piece of chocolate, closed her eyes, and savored it. Courageously, Amelia offered to go next.

The higher she climbed, the greater her sense of urgency. Far off in the distance, a somber sound ripped at her heart—the mournful song of humpback whales. Amelia stopped before reaching the attic and strained to listen. A smell of acrid smoke from a burning forest took over her senses and she began coughing. Tears streamed down her cheeks. Something was stirring inside her. Amelia couldn't imagine what was to come, but then looked up.

A transparent apparition of a man was waiting on the top step. Fright tore through Amelia. Her instinct was to turn and run, but she couldn't. She began to hyperventilate, grabbing at the banister to support her wobbly legs. The apparition hovered until Amelia regained composure. Trance-like, she followed the ghost into the turret.

§ § §

The house was quiet. Gwen remained seated, staring at the silver. She felt uneasy for Amelia, hoping she didn't encounter the same loud, alarming noises as Cassandra. Gwen tinkered with the tarnished pieces to pass time, admiring one or two interesting ones. From the corner of her eye, she caught a glint of light bouncing off a small, ornate tray with a heavy sculptured border. She picked it up to read the inscription of a wedding invitation, dated 1915.

Gwen put it down immediately. Memories of her own wedding invitations flooded her mind, as did the unexplained tension they evoked between her and her mother. That, her failed marriage, and so many other disappointments were the baggage she carried everywhere. She didn't need a reminder of those times.

Impatient, Gwen wandered aimlessly around the main floor. A door off the vestibule creaked open on its own, and a beam of sunlight landed directly at Gwen's feet. She sensed she was being summoned—but for what? Amelia was nowhere in sight, so Gwen trusted the beckoning ray and entered the circular, rose-colored library on the ground floor of the tower.

The light inside was blinding, and Gwen had to shield her eyes. She heard Amelia coming down the stairs and attempted to leave the library, but the door closed. To her horror, she heard the lock bolt on its own—holding her hostage. As hard as she tried, she could not get it to budge.

"Amelia! Ameliaaa! Get me out of here—I'm locked in the library!" she screamed.

Amelia reached the empty dining room. She did not hear Gwen's frantic shouts or her pounding on the library door. Assuming Gwen already left, she picked up her books to go.

There was a sudden quaking and loud roar in the room where Gwen was trapped. It sounded as if upper levels of the tower were caving in like a collapsing telescope. A force held Gwen against the wall. She could feel vibrations at every floor—the tower was turning itself inside out. Within seconds, Gwen was somewhere else not resembling the library at all. She had been transported to the turret by a supernatural force.

The room had a panoramic view of the entire town and harbor with the Victorian's red roof below. She could see Amelia's car leaving the driveway. Panic stricken, Gwen banged her fists against the windows, running from one to the other, trying to get Amelia's attention. Oblivious, Amelia drove away.

Gwen found herself right back in the dining room, sitting before the pile of tarnished silver. Her mind was fuzzy. It was difficult to remember what happened, and she wondered if it was merely a dream. Yet the shock she was feeling seemed real enough, and the rapid beating of her heart was unmistakable. Getting her wits together, she gathered her books from the table and hurried outside in time to see Daphne parking her car.

Dressed in beachwear, Daphne removed a cooler and folded aluminum chair from her trunk. "Hi. I'm surprised to see you here."

"I came for class along with Cassandra and Amelia. They left before me."

Daphne looked puzzled. "There was no class scheduled today."

"What do you mean? You had your chocolates on the table and taped a note to the fireplace mantle which told us to go..." Gwen stopped. The look on Daphne's face confirmed something was amiss.

Daphne lowered her voice. "I haven't made chocolate recently because it's too hot—and I surely didn't leave a note on the mantle."

Gwen couldn't argue. The bizarre afternoon already dwindled from her mind.

Daphne was anxious to get inside, said goodbye to Gwen, and went directly to the dining room. She sat at the table with a polishing cloth, frantically rubbing off tarnish, perturbed she had been excluded from the class.

"Have you forgotten this is my school?" Daphne hollered into the air.

She threw down the cloth and ranted throughout the house. This move by the ghost was something new, and she demanded an explanation. Daphne walked into the library. He was waiting for her, appearing as a faint glow against a bookcase.

"Are you taking over my school?" she raged. "You're just like Marc. I can never have anything of my own. You control it all!"

"Daphne, my dear one, I would never do such a thing."

"Then what happened here?" she demanded

"Shh…"

"Don't shush me. It doesn't work anymore."

"You must trust me. When the time is right and everything is in place, I need you to carry the love."

"What love are you talking about?"

"You'll remember."

Wednesday, August 13
There's no going back now. ~D~

CHAPTER 7

Holding On

AUGUST CONTINUED TO be oppressively hot, but few experienced it as a hardship more than Cassandra—her garden well dried up. It triggered childhood memories of drought on the farm, always resulting in deprivation during winter months. Gus delivered more bad news—the Cemetery Association would never approve an appeal to drill another well in that location. Cassandra reluctantly carried buckets of water from town spigots bordering the cemetery grounds, as hoses could not cross burial plots.

"Gus, I don't think I'll plant here again next year," she said, motioning her head down at the splashing pails in her hands. "Without easy access to water, I can't have a garden anymore."

Gus raised her spirits by transporting buckets in his pickup truck, but only when he was not busy digging another grave or maintaining the grounds. Mostly, she had to make do on her own. Cassandra longed for a better life, but spent all her free time toiling over the earth rather than dressing up for special dates. She thought of Daphne's turret while she worked, curious about what was up there and if Amelia and Gwen ever made it to the top.

Cassandra bristled from her recollection, visualizing the pile of tarnished silver and ridiculous note to meander through the dreary Victorian with awful and frightening sounds in the walls, as though she was an unwelcomed intruder. Returning was no longer an option. The school offered nothing of value to change her life. As if matters were not bad enough, the heat made it drudgery to maintain her garden.

By the next day, the temperature soared to a record breaking high. Cassandra drove along Main Street to get to her job. She approached Daphne's house and abruptly jammed on the brakes, coming to a halt. She banged her forehead against the steering wheel to clear her mind from what she saw taking place in the front yard.

A young mother with a toddler by her side was watering violet-blue wisteria wrapped around the porch pillars. Thick, lush ferns and giant hydrangea glistened from the drenching. A broad-shouldered, handsome young man with brown hair was sitting on the steps, smiling as the woman playfully sprayed the hose in his direction.

Cassandra broke into tears. The image was relevant—her dream— never to be. She wondered if it was heatstroke, or if she had been so brain-washed, she was torturing herself with an illusion of her own making. A car honked impatiently for her to move along. She took one last look, but the taunting scene was gone. Instead, a group of women wearing fancy summer dresses was lounging on porch chairs, sipping cool lemonade, chatting, and laughing. Cassandra suspected they were sharing tidbits of their superficial lives—so clean and perfect, while waiting for one of Daphne's fake classes to begin.

About to drive off, she looked at her young hands holding the steering wheel, raw from weeding and pruning her garden. They were discolored around cracks in her skin, and now calloused from carrying buckets of water across the cemetery each day.

That night, Cassandra collapsed into bed early, drawing her shades to block the last vestige of sunlight. A little fan pushed around a swirl of hot air, stirring dust in the room and making sleep elusive. A sense of unfairness simmered in her gut from the sight of pretentious indul-gences at Daphne's Victorian. She believed the dreamy vision on the lawn was a cruel trick of some kind.

Cassandra rose from her bed and walked across the room to a desk piled high with lists of people requesting food from a pantry she helped to supply. She picked up a pen to write a note, slipped into shorts and a sleeveless blouse, and left her tiny rented bungalow to deliver it.

CHAPTER 8

The Promise

THE TIMEWORN SCREEN door shuddered as the wind picked up. It distracted Daphne, who was watching the setting sun through the old Victorian's windows, heavily clouded over by layers of salty mist. She glanced down at beads of sand clinging to her feet from a walk on the beach. Late summer always drew her mind to melancholic thoughts, dreading the coming fall and winter months alone in the house. Daphne thought she saw her children running inside to get ready for their nightly ritual of baths, stories, and goodnight kisses. It was a moment of joy until she recognized it as wishful thinking.

The door slammed once again, and Daphne went into the kitchen to latch it. A small envelope had been partially slipped under the porch mat. She stooped to pick up the unexpected letter, fantasizing an invitation from a flesh and blood knight in shining armor, one who would carry her off to his castle. Daphne made her way into the parlor and sat in a favorite down-filled chair that enveloped every bit of her body. She read the message.

> *Daphne,*
> *I'm never coming back, ever again.*
> *Your fake school is just a cover-up for lazy people who daydream.*
> *They have nothing better to do.*
> *I'm sick of your ghost and all the weird stuff.*
> *You gave me false hope.*
> *Cassandra*

Tears rolled down Daphne's cheeks, dripping directly onto the ink, making some words barely readable. Despite the heat, Daphne comforted herself by pulling an old quilt up to her neck. The accusing letter devastated her. The school was not for daydreamers.

It was challenging for Daphne to be a teacher to less patient students wanting instant results. Teeny, tiny, almost imperceptible triumphs along the way were ignored. They assumed coincidences were random rather than the workings of the Invisible and allowed disappointment to influence their decisions instead. Some would completely give up. It was an entirely different issue when Daphne became the focus of their blame. Cassandra's letter was vexing, and Daphne wondered if she even wanted to continue teaching.

Her defensiveness soon gave way to a deeper level of internal conflict. Daphne rehashed the last fight she had with her husband, thirteen years before. Being steeped in anger at him, she paid no heed to red flag warnings of dangerous rip tides in front of the family's beach house. Running into the water, she was overtaken by the current. Miraculously, she was pulled to shore and resuscitated by an unknown hero. It all happened so fast, Daphne never fully understood what ensued.

Everything changed after that. Marc and the children hardly knew her. She barely knew herself. Marc blamed Daphne for the family breakup. She blamed him and his demanding ways, although she suspected something more profound was the reason. Daphne often felt adrift and fragmented, relying on the school and her business for stability. There was nothing more, except—the ghost. She wished she could be in Arthur's world to escape the emptiness of her own. Only when they were together did she feel whole—complete—like the symbol of the circle he showed her.

§ § §

Morning came and Daphne, who cried herself to sleep in the chair, stretched out from the awkward position. Her Wednesday afternoon class was starting in a few hours, and she needed to be in a better mental state. Without Cassandra, only Gwen and Amelia would likely attend. Heat—cold—time—day—haunted house—or far-out teacher were oft-used reasons for many to abandon their studies.

Daphne stood in the doorway of the dining room, recalling much of what had taken place around her big, well-loved table—life dramas, dreams, laughter, tears, insights, fears, grief, even meals, and many mysterious moments. Half smiling, she patted it gently like an old friend, wishing it could talk.

§ § §

Amelia and Gwen arrived for class and rearranged the various trinkets and books on the tabletop. They saw the empty chocolate dish. "Where did the chocolates go?" Amelia asked.

"I ate them," Daphne grumbled.

Gwen started rubbing her eyes. "Where's Cassandra?" Before anyone could answer her, she ran out the kitchen door. "I'll be back," she yelled, jumping into her car and driving off.

Gwen's sudden departure left Amelia alone with the sullen Daphne. "What's going on?" Amelia questioned.

Daphne held a folded piece of paper she twisted and turned, wanting to share its contents, but afraid it might open the floodgates of her private life. She bit her tongue and remained quiet. Amelia left the room to make a pot of coffee. Waiting for it to percolate, she patiently stood by the back door watching for Gwen to return and, hopefully, for Cassandra to show up.

A purplish mist formed in the front vestibule. Daphne saw it and looked away, being in no mood to be coaxed or seduced by Arthur. She stood to leave, but an immobilizing current went through her, temporarily thwarting her exit. The mist transformed to a vaporous sphere radiating the colors of fuchsia and lilac. It seemed to grow larger until a feathery plume fully engulfed Daphne.

Amelia broke the spell when she entered the dining room with clanking cups, saucers, and a pot of steaming coffee. Simultaneously, the mist faded, collapsing back into the nothingness from which it came, leaving Daphne midstep. The sound of a wind chime breezed through.

"Daphne, where are you going? Sit down and at least have a fresh cup of coffee."

Grudgingly, Daphne returned to her seat. She remembered Cassandra's note and frantically looked for it, turning over everything on the table.

"What on earth are you doing?"

Daphne ignored Amelia. Arthur had stolen the note, the contents of which made her want to close the school. She realized his power was intensifying.

§ § §

A spontaneous gust of wind picked up shortly after Gwen left the Victorian. An uncanny drop in temperature accompanied dark clouds rolling in from the harbor. Gwen looked at the blackened sky, wondering why she was heading straight up the hill toward the Hidden Arbor Cemetery, of all places. But with little hesitation, she drove right through the opened gates and down the road lined with majestic pine trees and hundreds of tombstones on either side. Gwen stopped short to avoid hitting a handsome gentleman in Victorian clothes, seen in her sepia vision. His dark, penetrating eyes were disconcerting as he stared in her direction. A scene appeared behind the spectral figure—a homestead from an earlier century.

The yard was alive with frolicking children and barking dogs. Women were sitting on the porch in rocking chairs, gossiping over tea and freshly baked bread. Men worked the fields, filling baskets with eggplants, beets, and cucumbers to bring in before dusk. Most prominent in Gwen's vision was a splendid arbor covered with blooming flowers cascading to the ground, like a delicate wedding veil made of intricate lace.

Gwen blinked, but everything disappeared. Spotting a woman tending a garden, she got out of her car to watch from behind a tree, careful not to attract attention. A truck sped down the road and parked near the garden. Franklin Port Pantry was written on the doors. The driver got out and took a huge sack of vegetables from the woman Gwen recognized as Cassandra. So surprised, Gwen didn't know what to do next.

The truck left, and Cassandra noticed Gwen peering around the tree. "How did you find me?" she called out, sounding irritated.

"I'm not sure," Gwen answered, walking closer.

"Daphne knows I'm not going to class anymore." Cassandra brushed off her dirty overalls. She picked up three empty buckets and shoved one into Gwen's hand as she passed her along the way to the water spigot. "As long as you're here, make yourself useful—then please leave."

"Why aren't you going to class anymore?" Gwen trailed after the young woman who appeared to be on a mission, let alone in a snit.

"Daphne didn't read my note to you and Amelia?" Cassandra questioned, thinking they both had another good laugh at her expense.

"I don't know about any note. Just as class began, something made me think to look for you. I can't explain it, but here I am."

"I've left the school for good," Cassandra stated resolutely. "I'm angry." She picked up the pace, leaving Gwen in the dust.

"Why are you angry?" Gwen huffed, trying to keep up.

"You guys laughed at me because I was too scared to go to the turret," Cassandra shouted back.

"You misunderstood us. It was just nervous laughter. And remember, we both encouraged you to try again."

Cassandra stopped walking and turned to give Gwen a piece of her mind, but a vague, tinkling wind chime already caught Gwen's attention. She could hear the distant sound of bubbling water. The man she almost hit with her car reappeared not far off.

"Who is that?" Gwen pointed at the figure.

"I don't see anyone," Cassandra answered sharply.

Gwen ignored what she realized was an apparition and continued. "Everyone gets upset for reasons they believe are true, but most things are not as they appear. You know this from Daphne's classes."

Cassandra started walking toward the spigots. Just hearing Daphne's name peeved her. Her mind was made up—she didn't appreciate anyone trying to change it now, especially after giving Daphne a nasty letter.

"Why are we carrying these buckets? Where are we going" Gwen groaned, exhausted.

"I need to get water—isn't it obvious?"

"Why not use the water pouring out from the pump by your garden?"

The rusted pump to the dried-up well was gushing water. Cassandra dropped her bucket and ran back to shut it off. In disbelief, she turned it on and off, on and off. "How can a bone dry well suddenly fill with water?"

"Things we don't understand happen all the time," Gwen replied. She offered to help finish watering the garden.

By then, it didn't take much for Cassandra to consider returning to the Victorian. Besides, she wouldn't run into that cute carpenter again if she stayed away. Apart from the phenomenon she just witnessed, seeing him was enough to swallow her pride. She could only hope Daphne didn't read the note to Amelia.

Before Gwen drove out the cemetery gates, she had an impulse to look back. Shadows of many people surrounded the pump. In a remote corner by old gravestones, the Victorian ghost briefly reappeared.

Both women tumbled through the Victorian's kitchen door and into class. Daphne reached over the table to lovingly squeeze Cassandra's hand to welcome her, holding tightly as though she would never let her go again.

§ § §

Daphne was preparing for nightfall when something prompted her to go into the dank basement. She twisted and pulled the brass doorknob, but the swollen basement door would not budge. It suddenly released, almost sending her flying. She turned on the light switch at the top of the stairs. The bulb blew out—the basement remained dark. With only a candle in hand, she made her way down. The old bricks forming the foundation were weeping their white mortar.

She went directly to a crusty metal box where a wood-burning tool was stored, then climbed back up the creaky stairs in a dream-like state. The cumbersome tool, wound with a black electric cord, was swinging in her hand with each step, like the sway of a lantern held by a lighthouse keeper.

Daphne positioned the candleholder on the oak table and waited for the tool to heat up. Without knowing what was to come, one letter at a time, on one side of the massive carved table, just under the tabletop so it could not be seen without looking for it, she burned these words:

I promise to foster student dreams,
Even if by curious means,
And by these words I shall abide.

She finished writing and put the tool down before going to the back door to see who was knocking. The additional words, *I am with you from the Other Side,* appeared on their own and flickered away.

CHAPTER 9

Second Thoughts

ALTHOUGH THE LESSON did not go as planned, each student certainly learned something if she looked for meaning beneath the experience. Cassandra took the greatest gamble, not in delivering a venomous note to Daphne, but by exposing her own vulnerability and returning after doing so, hoping for forgiveness. Leaving the school for the day, Cassandra decided to check the pump again. It was difficult to believe water flowed so abundantly, and she needed to assure herself it was not another daydream.

Gus was standing by her parents' gravesite when she arrived. "I knew you would be back before I locked the gates for the night." He smiled at the accuracy of his prediction.

Cassandra struggled to understand recent events. The school made her feel like a fish out of water, yet she did return. It seemed there was a mysterious force weaving itself in and out of each student's life. Cassandra was entangled in Daphne's web, like the rest of them, and was unsure why she was included. She couldn't even comprehend how Daphne forgave her for writing a nasty note.

Gus broke the silence between them. "Your well is running stronger than ever. It must have been a rock clogging it."

"Gus, something else is going on." Cassandra wondered if Daphne's ghost was responsible for the water flowing again—and why he would even bother with it. "Do you believe in ghosts?" she asked, looking straight into his eyes.

"Yes, I believe in all supernatural things—angels, ghosts, and you know—the man upstairs, above all."

Such conviction was unexpected. Cassandra hoped her hunch was wrong, but with the job Gus had, who would know better? They said their goodbyes and she left.

§ § §

Cassandra drove home along the northern road of Franklin Port, where an old lace factory was once the hub of the town's economy. Now it was a derelict building, having fallen into ruins when the town's industry shifted to the harbor. She considered herself fortunate to have a tiny place to rent on the mill's property. Of the fifty or so bungalows clustered together, only ten were habitable after years of neglect.

Cassandra crossed a tiny, screened-in porch. The summer furniture smelled of mildew, and she made a mental note to hose it down. A neighbor's dog came running her way, looking for a treat before she entered her humble abode.

The compact kitchen had an old refrigerator with layers of ice in the freezer—defrosting it meant more work. The steel-gray paint on the worn, wide-planked floors matched the peeling trim around the mill's hundreds of broken windows. In the center of the square room was a wood burning stove to keep her warm in winter, provided she stocked the bin outside with split logs. Cassandra threw down an armload of things and sighed, blaming herself for how her life was going.

Before cooking dinner, Cassandra stepped into the shower, crudely constructed with a cement base and curtain circling a rusty water head. She longed for a huge bathtub where she could completely immerse herself, but was grateful for the steady stream of water that night. She dried off, put on clean pajamas, and fixed a simple dinner.

Sitting alone at her small, wooden dining table with a chipped plate holding fresh food, Cassandra looked out the window at a few children playing on the bleak street, as though they were from another era. After dinner, she went straight to bed, being exhausted both physically and emotionally—but couldn't sleep.

She was feeling terribly guilty that, when she arrived at the Victorian with Gwen, the class went on as usual. Cassandra thought Daphne was owed an apology for the biting note. Once again, she got out of bed, dressed in shorts and a t-shirt, and drove straight to Daphne's house.

§ § §

Cassandra knocked at the back door and nervously waited for Daphne to ask who was there. Daphne invited her into the dining room. Cassandra saw the wood-burning tool and wondered why it was on the table, but she had something more urgent on her mind than to ask about it.

"What brings you here at this hour?" Daphne inquired.

"Well...uh...I want to apologize. I did something awful, and I'm feeling terrible. I don't understand why you aren't mad at me."

"Your note made me so upset, I thought it might be time to close the school," Daphne admitted.

"Oh no, I didn't mean what I said. Please don't close the school because of me. It's a very cool place...really."

"Cassandra, I felt hurt, angry, and insulted, but those are not the right emotions to act upon."

"So you can forget what I wrote?"

"Not quite, but I want to let it go so I won't carry it around to color everything else I do." Daphne touched Cassandra's hand. "I have a secret to tell you."

Cassandra pulled back, embarrassed, feeling unworthy of a secret.

"Most students who attend my classes are struggling with some form of anger or resentment over their past, the common roadblocks making dreams elusive. Like everyone, I have the same challenge. Our emotions create fear and bad habits that get in the way of all we do. I can only make my students aware of this. And at times, my students return the favor."

Cassandra started crying. "You're right. I'm angry."

"With me, if I may ask?"

"I was at first, but realized I'm still mad at my parents. My father died leaving the family in debt. Before my mother died, my brother moved, forcing me to deal with everything. I've had no time to make friends—and I'm broke. Yes, I'm angry—and resentful too. Why haven't you ever taught your students how to deal with this?" Cassandra was on the verge of again blaming Daphne for her frustrations.

"I do, but only when someone is ready will she hear the message. Anger and forgiveness are wrapped around each other. You just experienced the feeling of being forgiven. Can you pass it along to others?"

"I never thought to forgive anyone. I guess I tend to blame instead."

"Funny we should be talking about this. I have something for you." Daphne went into the kitchen and took a fresh batch of chocolates from the refrigerator. "You've never asked me about the images on my chocolates. I'm adding this new one for our class next week. It's a water drop." She held one up for Cassandra to see. "In dreams, water can symbolize washing away negativity."

Daphne handed the chocolate to Cassandra who closed her eyes, put it in her mouth, and let it melt. Since entering the school, this was the first time she set an intention. Moments later, Cassandra opened her eyes. "By the way, what does the moon image mean?"

"It represents the feminine, receptive side to us. The moon holds all the mysteries of love."

"How come you never told me what it meant when I kept eating all those moon chocolates?"

"You weren't curious until tonight."

Cassandra got up to leave, feeling optimistic. As she walked toward the door, she turned and asked in her little girl voice, "Daphne, may I please have a moon chocolate too?"

Wednesday, August 20
Forgiveness is a life force that can break through the hardened shell of the past. I had to learn it the hard way, just like my students. ~D~

CHAPTER 10

Waning and Waxing

OVER THE NEXT months, Cassandra kept busy harvesting her vegetables for the food bank. She took home the excess to can for herself. Fall presented another pressing matter—keeping warm in her bungalow. She loaded her car with twigs and broken branches found near the thicket to supplement cords of split wood brought to the small enclave of bungalows.

Women in her community, mostly married with children, showed up with wheelbarrows to greet the delivery truck. In the past, Cassandra would wait until no one was around to take her share from the woodpile. Joining the others for the first time, her attempt to make friends went well, and some expressed interest in learning how to can vegetables. Although happy for new relationships, Daphne's words about anger and forgiveness haunted Cassandra. Burdened by these emotions, moving forward was difficult. She knew it was time to revisit her childhood, once and for all.

§ § §

One chilly October morning, Cassandra psyched herself up for a trip to the rural farming community west of Franklin Port. She had no idea what became of the family land and house, but clearly remembered the last day she lived there after the death of her mother. The property was in default because of unpaid taxes and bank loans. At the eleventh hour, a buyer appeared and offered a deal where Cassandra could step away debt free, but would have no assets from the transaction. Left no other choice, she crammed her mother's car with the few remaining heirlooms and sadly said good bye to everything she knew.

Nearing her destination, Cassandra imagined a thriving farm and fresh coat of red paint on the barn, preparing herself for bittersweet feelings. Disoriented, she almost drove right past it. An explosion of upscale houses now took over the entire fifty acres. From the road, her only recognition of what remained was the majestic, weeping willow tree with her wooden swing hanging by ropes from a branch above. Behind it stood a faint resemblance of her childhood house — restored and landscaped with a sign in front, Sales Office. She turned onto the unfamiliar driveway, widened and curved. Cassandra's past unfolded before her, the source of pain and everything she hated. Her life could have been easier if she hadn't been desperate to take the first deal offered for the land.

Cassandra stepped into her living room converted to an office with desks. She told a salesman she would like to peek at the different models on display throughout the house. By herself in the kitchen, Cassandra's head filled with the recollection of shouting matches between her mother and father. Her older brother told her they could not fix their parents, they could only fix themselves.

As if just yesterday, she remembered her father repairing a leak in the roof and the tragedy of his death when he fell off the ladder. The seven years following were filled with hard work and despair. The death of her mother sealed the fate of the farm. Daphne was right, old memories were in her way.

Cassandra drove off, determined to leave the bad feelings behind — forever — thinking it would be simple. She hoped to get to Franklin Port in time for Daphne's evening class — one Daphne promised to be a humdinger.

§ § §

Amelia and Gwen entered the Victorian on time. They heard extraordinary music coming from the parlor. "What do you think this class is about?" Gwen asked.

"I don't know, but we're about to find out."

They walked through the vestibule and stood at the parlor's threshold. The room glowed with firelight from dozens of twinkling candles perched atop silver candelabras. In the center was a circle of seven striking women dressed in exotic costumes. Their hips were draped with strings of shiny beads and coins jingling their own rhythm with each circling motion.

The flames in the massive fireplace roared and crackled while two women sat in a corner playing a hand-made flute and drum. The colors, sounds, and burning incense left Amelia and Gwen spellbound. It appeared they had walked into a ceremonial dance class, honoring the ancient ways.

Upon seeing her students arrive, Daphne rose from the apple-green, silk couch and opened the heavy, velvet drapery hanging over leaded-glass windows. "Come with me." She gestured for Amelia and Gwen to follow her to an adjacent room.

A rack filled with costumes stood in the center—sheer harem pants, long skirts, veils, hip scarves, and jangling accessories for ankles, wrists, and necks. Daphne encouraged them to change their clothing and join the circle. Amelia and Gwen were beside themselves, giggling like school-girls and throwing bits of costumes over each other, deliberately delaying their participation.

"This beats plastic bags," Gwen said, tongue-in-cheek, pulling on a gauzy skirt.

"Bags would be better—you can't see through them." Amelia roared with laughter, searching for a top to cover her midriff.

Feeling self-conscious, they dragged each other into the parlor. Amelia was the first to enter the circle of dancers, allured by the hypnotic drum-beat. She didn't find it hard to be swept away. Gwen was relieved to see Cassandra arrive. She could avoid the activity by helping Cassandra pick out a costume.

"What's all this?" Cassandra asked, eyeing Gwen's outfit. "I've had a tough day and I'm not into dancing, especially if I have to change my clothes."

"Neither am I, but all the more reason for us to let our hair down and have fun," Gwen said, unraveling Cassandra's tight braid down her back.

Reluctantly, Cassandra dressed in a costume. She let Gwen brush her honey-colored hair. It flowed in soft waves and framed her beautiful face. When Cassandra saw her reflection in a glass curio cabinet, she adorned herself with jingling jewelry and joined the circle, feeling radiant.

§ § §

Responding to Daphne's invitation, Jacquelyn arrived for the class. Unwilling to enter, she stood outside the Victorian, observing the goings on through a window. She saw a young woman with flowing hair join a circle of dancers. Jacquelyn reached to the nape of her neck where her platinum hair was tightly bound in a ponytail. She yanked it out from the band—wishing she had the gumption to go inside and claim the center of attention.

It was as though Jacquelyn was in a fine theater, watching dancers on a stage. The room's muted glow bounced off glittery costumes. She was feeling left out. Amelia's eyes caught Jacquelyn, and she motioned for her to come inside. Jacquelyn ignored her. Uncomfortable memories surfaced, and she heard her father's stern words, as if just spoken. "Jacquelyn, forget your delusions about auditioning for the high school musical. You were born to be a scientist. You must keep up your grades to prepare for college. How can you study if you go to a useless audition?"

Her father's voice played over again in her head until she broke into tears. She agonized over what career she would have chosen had her father not decided for her. Seeing the women dancing, she wanted to be a part of the circle, but got back into her car and stormed off. Her father won again.

§ § §

The musicians' tempo quickened, and the dancers twirled unceasingly, shaking their hips to the drumbeat. At the height of the dance, minds could open up to Universal Knowledge. Enraptured by music, dancers knew anything might happen.

Gwen jumped away as the circle reached its fullness. Amelia noticed, but was powerless to break free from the energy. The dancers strengthened it by swirling veils around their bodies and throwing back their heads in joyful laughter. Suddenly, the fireplace flames burned down to a few embers, and they stopped dancing. Only two candles remained lit. Everyone left the Victorian except Amelia, Gwen, and Cassandra. They grabbed Daphne's quilts to keep warm as cold air crept into the room.

"I'll be going away for six weeks, starting mid-December. We'll still have classes until then," Daphne announced.

"Where are you going?" Amelia asked.

"I'm spending the holiday at Mount Hope Lodge, a ski resort."

"Nice," Amelia mused. "Have you ever been there before?"

"Yes, too many times to remember. I'll be meeting my childhood friend, Sophia, and my daughter, Nancy."

"I'm so happy you and Nancy will be together during the holidays." Amelia smiled, knowing how much Daphne missed her daughters, both still living in Europe.

"Thank you, I'm looking forward to it. And I'm inviting the three of you to join me for a few days after the New Year, if you can get away. It's my treat, of course."

"That's a tempting invitation," Amelia remarked.

Gwen remained uncharacteristically quiet.

"Well, there's still time. Everyone can decide later," Daphne suggested, noticing Gwen's odd lack of response. Not waiting for either Gwen or Cassandra to comment, Daphne climbed the winding staircase for the night, leaving them to stay behind as long as they wanted.

§ § §

Cassandra was the last to change back into her clothes, savoring how sultry she felt. Being so spontaneous, she wondered if her childhood pain actually was behind her. "Why did Daphne invite us to a class like this?" she asked, braiding her hair into its usual style.

Amelia turned to Cassandra. "Are you kidding? Look at yourself. You're like a different person—and so are we. Daphne must have realized we were ready for this experience."

Cassandra did feel different, pretty for the first time in her life. She released the braid and let her hair freely sway across her back.

"Did I see somebody else show up while we were dancing?" Gwen asked Amelia.

"Yes, it was Jacquelyn, the woman who sang the loudest at Daphne's Fourth of July party."

"What woman are you talking about?" Gwen asked.

"You know—the blonde in the skimpy outfit. When she realized I saw her standing outside the house tonight, she ran to her car and drove off."

"Where was she standing?" Gwen probed.

"On the driveway, looking in the window," Amelia answered, sounding puzzled by Gwen's questions.

"Oh…I thought I saw someone show up in the middle of the circle, not on the driveway."

"In the middle? Now I'm confused—who did you see in the middle?"

"I don't know. Don't mind me."

"Is that why you left the circle?" Amelia asked.

"I don't know," Gwen said again, gesturing with her hand for the conversation to stop.

Amelia closed the parlor draperies before they left the house. Gwen, however, had forgotten her purse and went back inside. A cold breeze crossed her face. She searched for the purse in dark rooms, feeling uncomfortable by herself. Upon finding it, a message illuminated in golden light across the wall, then disappeared. It was one Daphne spoke of often.

57

Make peace with your circumstances.

CHAPTER 11

ESP

GWEN SLEPT POORLY, repeatedly awakening in a cold sweat, her red hair matted from tossing and turning. It was similar to many fitful nights she remembered as a child.

Back then, she had recurring dreams about holding one end of a cord that went through a solid wall. Her little hands unsuccessfully tried making an opening in the partition to see who was holding the cord on the other side.

Another wall had appeared in that evening's dance circle, but was not opaque like in her childhood dreams—it was transparent. Shocked, Gwen saw herself holding the cord on the other side.

Gwen couldn't make sense of her visions, old and new, as long as the strange episodes during her childhood remained unresolved. People claimed to have seen her in one location, when she was actually elsewhere. Beginning in grade school, those mysterious occurrences happened frequently. Once she was in her teens, there were consequences. Her mother spotted her roaming the streets when school was in session. No matter how insistent Gwen was of her innocence, she was punished. A thorny relationship resulted between them. Not knowing what was real, Gwen lost her confidence.

The final blow to their mother-daughter bond was the day the doorbell rang with a special delivery—Gwen's printed wedding invitations. Her mother excitedly opened the box, examined the contents, and burst into uncontrollable tears. There was a printer's error. The bride's name should have read Gwendolyn Ann instead of Gracie Ann.

Gwen's mother hurled the box into the snow-covered yard. Her overreaction was bewildering, since it was an easily correctable mistake. Gwen retrieved the invitations and went directly to the print shop to complain. She was embarrassed to see her name was indeed correct.

During her marriage, Gwen began developing heightened extra sensory perception—intuitive knowing. Her ability to locate missing objects and people increased. Gwen's husband belittled her unusual talent. Only after they divorced did she realize he was afraid of being caught in compromising situations.

Gwen attended Daphne's school to embrace her psychic gifts. The night's dance circle jarred memories of her turret experience the past summer. Now recalling her terror when trapped in the library, she couldn't imagine having forgotten it.

Gwen was held by a force against a curved wall. The room began whirling around and around, propelling her upward, like a tornado's vortex. When she opened her eyes, she was steeped in glowing amber light. Dizzy and frightened, she sat on a bench before a full-length mirror. Gwen thought she was seeing her own reflection and leaned forward to touch the mirror's surface. The image didn't move. She sat in frozen astonishment. The form grew faint, revealing other images barely discernible through the haze—mountains with a purple sky, a flat, carved stone, and sweet alyssum leading to entwined, blue morning glories with a profusion of white baby's breath. Gwen had no idea what any of it meant.

A male voice spoke from nowhere. "Gwendolyn, I need your help."

The next scene in the turret's mirror catapulted her back to Daphne's Fourth of July party. Once again, she witnessed a young boy falling off the dock, but this time, Gwen saw more. A man wearing a white medical coat rushed out the Victorian's back door. In an instant, he pulled the boy from the water—just before the oncoming schooner could have killed them both.

"Who is that child?" Gwen cried out.

The voice responded. "Find him. Help him. Then I'll have a gift for you."

"Find who…help who…what gift?" An arrow floated across the mirror and disappeared into thin air.

Gwen's past and present were coalescing. Her double in the mirror was the same figure she saw in the dance circle, and the likes of which haunted her childhood. If only she could understand what was bubbling up to the surface for her to know.

CHAPTER 12

Walls that Talk

AS THE WEATHER turned colder, changing leaves were a harbinger of autumn's liveliness. Thaddeus Fulton invited his wife, Amelia, to meet him for dinner at the Port Empress Inn, an establishment of fine dining with an authentic historical atmosphere. In recent times, the building was refurbished to its original stateliness by a restaurateur from the city, Charles Hinds.

Amelia entered the restaurant at 6 o'clock sharp, escaping a damp fog engulfing the village. Knowing her husband would not be along for another fifteen minutes, she took a seat in the lobby near the front desk.

"Are you waiting for the rest of your party?" the hostess politely asked.

"Yes, my husband will be here shortly."

"Would you like me to escort you to the cocktail lounge to wait?"

"No thank you, I'm fine."

"May I suggest you enjoy the documents hanging on the walls? They trace the history of this building." The hostess pointed to an array of plaques, framed pictures, and newspaper articles.

Amelia stood to get a better look, drawn to photographs taken during the building's extensive renovations. "What was this place before it became the Port Empress Inn?" she asked.

"It was a private home, built a long time ago."

"How did it fall into such disrepair?"

"By being abandoned for decades," the young woman answered.

Amelia recognized its similarities to Daphne's Victorian, but it was built on a grander scale with greater attention to detail. "Who would ever abandon an architectural showplace like this?"

"The past owner died in the house," the hostess whispered. "It remained empty and deteriorated over time. Because there was bad blood between the owner and his brother, I'm guessing the estate was tied up with legalities. Check out the newspaper articles about their sibling rivalry and public fights," she said, happy to share gossip, however old it might be.

As Amelia sauntered toward earlier documents, she heard the hostess greet Charles Hinds, the current owner. Amelia turned to get a better look. He was a fit, older man with silvery-brown hair and deep blue eyes. Something about his demeanor conveyed honesty and openness. On more than one occasion, Amelia was certain she'd seen this man leaving Daphne's house and wondered what connection they had to each other.

Still waiting for her husband, Amelia returned to reading articles about a contentious relationship between two brothers. Their names jumped out, Simon Wake and Dr. Arthur Wake. Amelia bit her lip, trying to wrap her mind around this story and the little she knew about Arthur, the ghost in Daphne's house. "Miss," she called to the hostess once Mr. Hinds left for the bar. "Was Simon Wake the owner of this property?"

"Yes. There's a plaque with his name to your left," she answered, shuffling her menus into order to seat two customers waiting at the bar for a table.

Amelia was intrigued. Two iconic houses in the same village were once owned by brothers who hated each other. She assumed Simon had more money, judging by the immensity of his Victorian. Moving along the wall of photos, one of them startled her. It was an impressive schooner docked behind Simon's waterfront mansion, a vessel she had seen before, but couldn't place where.

She continued studying the chronicles. One event was so poignant it made her mouth drop, a narrative written by an observer who awaited the 1865 arrival of a ship, the Port Empress, bringing home Civil War soldiers. Protected behind a glass frame was an aged photograph of people on shore, cheering and waving lanterns for the ship's crew to see on the overcast day. But the homecoming was not to be. The caption beneath the picture reported a sudden raging squall, sending the ship to an underwater grave. There were no survivors. According to the story, those on the dock huddled in anguish. Recovered bodies were temporarily placed in a refuge station—the very spot on which Simon built his house decades later.

Amelia winced, imagining stacked bodies where she was standing. Her toes curled in her shoes. Disregarding the feeling, she checked her watch—6:30. "Ugh," Amelia muttered, irritated by her husband's lateness.

The hostess returned to the lobby. "I believe your husband might already be at the bar. Does he have salt and pepper hair?" she asked Amelia.

"Yes, his hair is graying, but I didn't see him pass me."

"He's been here all this time—and with a guest."

"No, wrong party, we have a table for two reserved, not three."

"Oh…I apologize."

Hearing piano music begin, Amelia was drawn to the bar. Thad was already there—enjoying himself alongside a lithe, young blonde. "So what have we here?" Amelia hissed. Her husband was smartly dressed after a big-deal board meeting. It struck Amelia how well he wore the image of success. She was never before threatened by the idea other women might also find him attractive, but obviously, this one did.

Amelia was glad she took extra time to fix herself up. Patting her hair in place, she tapped Thad on the shoulder—clenching her teeth. He spun around on the bar stool with a huge grin on his face, as did the attractive young thing sitting next to him. It was none other than Jacquelyn Daye.

"Oh hi, Amelia," Jacquelyn sweetly spoke, cozying up to Thad. "I've never seen you here before."

"You two know each other?" Thad wondered, embarrassed by Jacquelyn's advances.

"That we do, from Daphne's school," Jacquelyn grinned.

"No, Jacquelyn, only from Daphne's party. I've never seen you take a class," Amelia corrected. "But I do see you've met my husband."

Jacquelyn squinted, looking back and forth at the two of them. "This man is your husband?" she asked, disbelievingly.

Thad, who found himself in an uncomfortable situation, responded to his wife's glare. "Hun, I arrived early and was waiting for you." Just then, the hostess announced their table was ready. Thad awkwardly looked at Jacquelyn. "Would you like to join us?"

One could cut the air with a knife. Jacquelyn, drink in hand, slid off the bar stool. Dressed in high heels and a tight skirt, she swayed her hips while walking alongside the hostess who led them into another room. Amelia trailed behind, trying not to be rude. They were seated at a linen covered table with a crystal vase of red roses in the center. No one noticed the breathtaking harbor views outlined by soaring hills twinkling with lights.

"Do you come here often?" Amelia asked Jacquelyn.

"All the time."

Jacquelyn was eyeing Charles Hinds standing by the bar. She twirled her hair with two fingers, as if to entice him. In no time, Charles brought menus and a courtesy pot of tea. He smiled at everyone, but his eyes lingered on the temptress. Amelia looked at Thad, but he was too absorbed in watching the dynamics to notice her.

"It's nice to see you again, Jacquelyn." To Amelia and Thad he added,

"My name is Charles Hinds. Your waiter will be here in a moment to take your order. If there is anything you need, I'll be happy to help you."

"I'll bet," Amelia sighed, watching Jacquelyn cling to his every word. Amelia wanted to laugh, having no patience for such antics. Throughout dinner, she buried her discomfort under superficial conversation, until Jacquelyn unexpectedly riled her up.

"Daphne told me you're also in science. I don't know why you, of all people, would go to her school. It's a strange fantasy land."

"If you feel that way, what brought you to the Victorian?" Amelia countered.

"When I heard Daphne's library talk about thoughts creating reality, I wondered what kind of simple-minded people fall for such nonsense. I accepted her invitation to the Fourth of July party specifically to meet you, but was distracted by the crazy thing happening on the dock and all the other stuff—including some boat. Was there a boat, or was everything staged with special effects? What is going on there?"

"Let's just say it's entertaining. I admit I haven't figured it out myself. But Jacquelyn, I know you came to the Victorian during a ceremonial dance class and never entered the house. Why did you bother returning if you found the activities so absurd?"

"Because I hate my life...and...I don't know how to change it."

Thad excused himself and headed to the bar until dessert was served, feeling guilty for ruining what was to be a surprise for his wife.

"We all have adversity—what do you hate about your life?" Amelia was taken off guard by Jacquelyn's succinct answer.

"Everyone in my family is a scientist and expected me to follow suit. Yet my job is still not good enough to satisfy my father. If I had the guts, I would have followed my dream and gone into theatre instead. A part of me is dead."

Jacquelyn's honesty softened Amelia's attitude. "You do have a beautiful voice. I heard you sing at Daphne's party."

"Do you really think so?" Jacquelyn lapped up the admiration.

The waiter brought dessert menus. Jacquelyn twirled her hair as she ordered, staring at the bar. She was beautiful but seemed lost. Amelia looked to see who captured Jacquelyn's attention. It was Charles Hinds again.

"Why do you keep looking at the owner?" Amelia asked.

Jacquelyn didn't respond.

"I've seen Charles Hinds at Daphne's house."

"He visits Daphne?" Jacquelyn asked sharply. "Why would he do that?"

"I don't know. Daphne has lots of people coming and going," Amelia spoke, wondering why it even mattered. "Jacquelyn, what's upsetting you?"

Jacquelyn revealed a long series of disappointments. She wanted things to be different, but was resistant to change. She considered Daphne's school, but her father's words continued to influence her decision. "Amelia, how did you get from science to this…uh…magical thinking?" Jacquelyn dared to ask.

Amelia took a deep breath. "I was going through a difficult time, mired in the everyday drudgery of life, trapped by the same thoughts over and over. Something remarkable happened defying all explanation and logic. I saw the world operating differently and I wanted to understand what shifted. Like you, I met Daphne, and she also invited me to study in her school."

"And you sit there with candles, incense, and all Daphne's weird goings on as a way to figure it out?"

"I do, happily, and with chocolate." She gestured outward and added, "The mysterious is in everything—even in science. What is the space in and around atoms which make up physical matter?"

"I don't know," Jacquelyn answered, stunned by Amelia's question.

"It's the great unknown, where everything unexplained waits to be understood or experienced once we tap into it. Daphne's school holds the key."

Jacquelyn felt a soft brushing across her ankles. She peered under the table, yet found nothing but spotless, old wooden floors. "What the hell?" Frightened by something invisible stroking her, she frantically swatted around her feet.

"Maybe you're being touched by a ghost," Amelia half jested, remembering what she read in the lobby.

"How can you possibly be talking about science and then jump to ghosts? Don't be ludicrous," Jacquelyn scolded.

"Obviously, something you can't see is under the table."

Thad returned with the restaurant's owner. "Is everything all right?" Charles was nervous. This was not the first time a patron was frightened in his establishment. Being at the mercy of entities beyond his control, Charles never knew when they might strike again.

Jacquelyn felt a crawling tingle moving up her legs. She had enough, grabbed her purse, and ran off. Calling after her, Amelia suggested she read the Inn's history on her way out. It was the perfectly timed moment for Amelia. Not only were ghosts driving her point home, but they sent her party crasher out the door, as well.

After dessert, Thad revealed his good news. "Hun, I've wanted to tell you something all night. I know you're going to be thrilled."

"How could anything possibly thrill me more than spending the evening with you and that maddening woman?" Amelia asked with a sarcastic tone.

"I got a huge bonus, and we're going to receive a tidy little sum in December."

"You're right, Thad. I'm thrilled."

CHAPTER 13

Autumnal Abundance

J ASON, I WAS wondering if you might be able to stay in my house for a few weeks this winter," Daphne interrupted her contractor, who was painting the dining room walls in preparation for her annual harvest banquet.

"With you, my Lady?" he said, bowing and sweeping his arm as though removing a cap.

"Silly," Daphne replied, enjoying his playfulness. "Seriously, I'm going away for a period of time—one of those trips—and need you to watch over the house."

"I'm happy to oblige. I'll have the place to myself to entertain some young maiden in your castle. You can count on me."

"And Jason, I do expect you to attend the banquet. Please come early to light the fire outside and roast chestnuts for the guests." With that, Daphne went about her business decorating other rooms while Jason finished painting.

§ § §

Jason Wells was a restless, carefree sort, a guy's guy whose line of work suited him. He had the freedom to pursue pretty ladies who fell head over heels for his rugged good looks and tousled brown hair. A part of him wanted to settle down, but the right woman, one who could ground him, never seemed to come along.

He was the son of Daphne's dearest childhood friend, Sophia, who became pregnant at the age of fifteen after one night of reckless passion the summer she worked at a sleep-away camp. The end of the season bonfire attracted a number of older boys from across the lake, and throwing caution to the wind, Sophia slipped away with one of them. They stole each other's heart. He told her she was a beautiful Goddess he would remember forever, but they never so much as knew each other's names.

Nine months later, Sophia promised herself she would provide her newborn son with his father's last name. Finding him had been an ongoing effort relying upon Daphne's psychic skills for clues. Whenever Daphne was beckoned out of town, Sophia followed, always hopeful it was another lead. In Daphne's heart, she knew Jason would be united with his father someday, because now she sensed her ghost was helping the process along.

§ § §

The afternoon of the banquet arrived. Daphne invited her students, neighbors, business associates, and even new acquaintances she met during the week of preparation. Guests entered through the huge front doors, carrying homemade dishes with scrumptious aromas.

"Come in and introduce yourselves to anyone you don't know," Daphne said, taking their food offerings to the dining room.

Everyone stopped to stare at a life-sized statue prominently placed in the vestibule for the occasion. It was a classic image of a nude woman emerging from bathing and drying her graceful legs with a draped towel. Daphne adorned the figure with fine strings of a thousand tiny white lights so it seemed enshrouded in cosmic mist. It was her way of giving thanks to her first night in the house. She couldn't care less if guests thought it odd.

Upholstered period chairs and small tables covered in fine cloth with golden weave were scattered around the downstairs rooms. Candles were everywhere. Cut glass teardrops decorated the fireplace mantels and door lintels. The massive dining table, with freshly polished silver, was set for a queen and her court.

Charles brought a jug of mulled cider from the Inn. He poured the hot liquid into glass mugs with a crystallized, honey-dipped cinnamon stick and handed them out. When he reached Jacquelyn, it took her by surprise. She was freezing, having been in the cold flirting with Jason, who she just met over the outdoor fire. Had she known Charles was at the party, she would have come inside sooner and also dressed differently from the drab, thick woolen clothing concealing her toned body. To regain her composure, Jacquelyn teased him, stroking his hand when taking the mug. Charles smiled.

Jason did a double take when Cassandra arrived—not that she was such a refined beauty, but something about her once again caught his interest. He watched her walk up the steps and through the front doors.

Cassandra handed Daphne a homemade, deep-dish apple pie before throwing her coat over the pile on the mirrored hallstand. Jacquelyn stood in a nearby corner watching her.

"This smells heavenly," Daphne commented, inhaling the spicy fragrance. "And you look so lovely in your charcoal-gray dress."

Cassandra blushed, feeling ill at ease when she noticed another young woman staring at her and listening in. She smoothed her dress self-consciously.

Daphne rang a small bell, calling her guests to dinner. The sideboard labored under corn pudding, bread stuffing, and assorted vegetable bakes. In the center was the main dish, roasted and carved to perfection, surrounded by trays filled high with steaming hot, popover biscuits. Jacquelyn rushed to sit next to Charles, while Cassandra claimed the chair on her other side.

Jacquelyn waved Cassandra away. "This seat is saved, find another one." She grimaced, taking notice of Cassandra's calloused hands with short, ragged nails.

Daphne diverted the incident by offering Cassandra a chair across the table next to a dashing young man. "Everyone, I'd like to introduce Miles Goode. He's our town's producer and playwright in residence for the winter theater extravaganza."

Jacquelyn squirmed. She couldn't believe a producer was in the house and sitting next to that girl.

Jason walked inside and took the empty seat next to Jacquelyn. He reached behind her to shake hands with Charles, exchanging a brief greeting. Seeing Cassandra, he stood up and leaned over the table to shake her hand, holding it longer than necessary.

"Finally," he mouthed. The chandelier twisted back and forth for all to see, but it went unnoticed.

"There's a baby in your future," Gwen jokingly announced, having seen an image of an infant, followed by an arrow shooting through time and space.

Jacquelyn scowled while the others laughed at Gwen's fanciful and romantic words. They held their silver goblets high and toasted the couple. Not caring if Gwen's prediction was accurate, the lightheartedness launched the party—and fueled Jacquelyn's jealousy.

Daphne asked everyone to close their eyes and give thanks for the goodness in their lives, opening the way for more. Cassandra dared to raise her head and steal a look at Jason, who was looking back.

The meal began, wine flowed, and lively conversations filled the night. Once everyone was stuffed, Daphne encouraged them to find a comfortable nook somewhere in the house, while she cleared the table and prepared for dessert and coffee.

The women gathered in the parlor; the men made their way to what had been Dr. Wake's library to talk about their business ventures, politics, and the war. It was the only place in the house where Daphne had no control. Against her wishes, they smoked and sipped brandy. No matter how many times she hired Jason to paint the walls a deep rose, the room refused to release its masculine essence—it still belonged to Dr. Arthur Wake.

Jacquelyn, who was proud to have broken into a man's professional world, followed the men to the library. She stopped short at its entrance. "What the hell is going on? This is a crazy house. Why can't I get through the damn doorway when it's wide open?" She flailed her arms against an Invisible energy blocking her. The men watched, puffing on their cigars, amused. Mortified, Jacquelyn reluctantly joined the women in time to hear Cassandra complaining about another winter fast approaching, explaining how she couldn't supply the pantry with fresh food.

Jacquelyn perked up. "What are you—a freaking, damn saint?"

Cassandra countered Jacquelyn's arrogance. "I help single women with children who don't have enough to eat. Returning soldiers also need the food bank. Do you care about anyone besides yourself?"

The men, particularly Jason, heard the heated dialogue and observed from the library. Jacquelyn absolutely had to have the last word, the coup de gras. She took center stage for herself. "Nobody cares about your stupid little mission. People should take more control over their lives."

"Stuff happens," Cassandra fired back.

Jacquelyn couldn't help herself. She went over the top with her performance, gesturing with beautifully manicured, well moisturized hands— unable to carry a bottle of wine from her car for the hostess. "You stay a goody two shoes, but take a look at what it's doing to your hands— they're ugly!" Jacquelyn sneered.

Cassandra's face blanched and tears welled, freely running down her cheeks. She was done, finished, drained of the will to respond again. She grabbed her coat, leaving without a goodbye to anyone.

Jason stepped outside. "Cassie, come back," he shouted from the front porch. "Cassie, don't go."

Cassandra stopped, feeling tugged. She couldn't fathom how he would call her a name only her mother ever used, but she felt so humiliated, she kept going.

Jason returned to the party, looking despondent. Jacquelyn was floored by his apparent interest in Cassandra. She couldn't make sense out of why he would pursue a bumpkin over her.

Daphne carried a tray of French pastries into the parlor. The best of the night was yet to come, and the men joined the ladies. Daphne lowered the lights and sat on a tufted stool, then took out a hand drum and began a rhythmic beat. Instantly, everyone's eyes focused on the balcony where a dance troupe, quietly getting ready during dinner, began descending the stairs.

Twenty beautiful women in colorful costumes of long skirts and jingling coin belts accompanied Daphne's drumming with finger cymbals. The performers snaked their way like a serpent, following the first two who held candles in each hand. Moving seamlessly, the group wove single file through the tables where guests sat with rich desserts.

Jacquelyn was speechless. Once again, she was the audience rather than the center-stage attraction. Charles was captivated by the theatrical diversion, while Jason paced back and forth, hoping Cassandra would return, paying no attention to the entertainment before him. Both men ignored Jacquelyn, as though she and her gorgeous self didn't exist.

No one cared when Jacquelyn hightailed out the door to leave for home. More importantly, she missed out on Miles inviting everyone to audition for his current play. She ruined her own opportunity. That was as plain as anyone could see—just as plain as the heavy woolen clothing she wore.

§ § §

After the last guest left, Amelia was alone in the kitchen with Daphne. "What do you make of Cassandra and Jacquelyn tonight?" she asked.

"When anyone exits a door, they automatically walk through another, bringing the same, self-sabotaging patterns which set up a repeat situation. Nothing changes until he or she becomes aware," Daphne answered, putting away the final piece of silver.

The countless lights surrounding the statue in the vestibule repeatedly turned on and off, like a twinkling, star-filled galaxy. On cue, the Universe was agreeing with Daphne.

71

Sunday, November 16

The web is woven, but two strands lack stability unless a major shift in thinking takes place. Then they will realize how utterly stunning this night was—as if showered with gifts, rather than assaulted by mean-spirited words. Eventually, all will understand the connection of each life experience more clearly. What lies in the space, free from human influence, is patiently waiting to be discovered. ~D~

CHAPTER 14

Cold

CASSANDRA LEFT THE party, enraged. Daphne's house receded in her car's rear view mirror—its glow disappearing once she turned the corner. Her confrontation with Jacquelyn, for all to see, goaded her into wrestling with her past—again. Plummeting into emotional darkness, Cassandra dreaded going back to her bungalow.

Arriving home to the bleakness of the lace factory's ruins, the pockets of dim light from the few remaining shanties seemed to be mocking her. They were in sharp contrast to the radiance of Daphne's Victorian. A stray dog with a terrier face sat shivering by the door. He stood up, hesitated, and wagged his tail for an invitation to be warmed by the wood stove. His eyes were fixed on hers. She opened the door and lingered, allowing him to enter.

The dog let her wipe him down with a towel, studying her tentatively. Cassandra watched him avoid making any mistakes resulting in his falling from her good graces. She likened it to when her mother cowered during her father's tirades. Having sworn she would never do that, it gave her the strength to defend herself at the party.

Cassandra was distracted doing simple chores, trying to subdue childhood memories and rationalize her behavior—but to no avail. "Jacquelyn started it—just like dad always did. But I showed her a thing or two!" she told the little dog.

She patted his head to assure him he was safe. The animal returned the kind action, licking her tear-soaked cheeks. For a split second, Cassandra's heart opened up, and the hollow space filled with a rush of loving compassion. She became interconnected with everyone, including Jacquelyn. It finally registered—no one else was to blame for her unhappiness. Like her brother said, she could only fix herself.

Cassandra undressed, neatly putting away the clothes she wore. Her image in the dresser mirror changed into someone she might learn to love. Slipping into warm night clothes, thoughts of Jason flooded her mind.

She remembered him shaking her hand and their eyes connecting. "He called me Cassie," she said in a whisper.

Cassandra climbed into bed and pulled up the blankets. The dog waited, hoping for another invitation. She lifted the covers, calling him by his new name, Amigo. Love swallowed them both and they were buried in the warm bed every night thereafter.

§ § §

Jacquelyn had enough torment from Daphne's parties. Her car screeched out the Victorian's driveway and sped down Main Street toward her modern townhouse in a sophisticated new development. The foyer chandelier was ablaze with light as she stepped into her immaculate residence, stooping to pick up an interesting circular pushed through the mail slot while she was out.

One would surmise Jacquelyn was indifferent to the night's events as she went through her usual evening routine, unaffected. She often provoked others, but blamed them for the unpleasant outcomes, denying all responsibility. Tonight was no different. Wanting the undivided attention of both Jason and Charles, nothing irritated her more than being upstaged by another woman. Jacquelyn assessed Jason as being on the make and figured she should save him the seat next to her. However, someone else captured the spotlight. Jacquelyn's insane jealousy began when she first saw Cassandra at the ceremonial dance. The banquet only fueled the fire, making her wonder why such an annoying girl was in Daphne's circle in the first place.

She turned on her stereo to listen to a favorite opera, poured herself some expensive red wine, and kicked off her shoes. She rested her legs atop her austere chrome and glass coffee table and leaned back against the white leather couch. Jacquelyn spent the night listening to music, unresponsive to the opera's sad tale of betrayal and love lost as it resounded throughout sterile rooms. Before going to bed, she put away the bottle of cheap wine she forgot to give Daphne.

CHAPTER 15

The In-Between-Space

AMELIA LEFT DAPHNE'S banquet, hoping her husband had already returned from work. Reflecting upon the unsettling incidents at dinner, she appreciated Thad's steadfastness even more. Being preoccupied, she made a wrong turn, finding herself on a deserted road hugging the eastern shore of the harbor.

Amelia heard a wind chime tinkling, and her senses heightened. She noticed a salt-water eroded house along the beach. It was tucked away behind swaying, dried-up reeds, with a FOR SALE sign in front. The property had an otherworldly glow in the beams of her headlights, providing a clear view. She stopped the car to check out a two-story building that no doubt endured the harbor's history for over a century.

A second structure nearer to the shoreline had a sign over its door, FIRST HARBOR SCHOOL. Amelia figured it might have been the area's original schoolhouse. Intuitively, she knew something important was going on and trusted it would be revealed in time. But for now, Amelia was happy to find her way back to the main road.

§ § §

Thaddeus Fulton greeted his wife as she melted into the tranquility of their cottage. He lit the fireplace to heat the room. The larger-than-life energy from Daphne's party soon dissipated into tender silence. Amelia curled up on the couch next to her husband.

"So, was our friend, Jacquelyn, at the party?" Thad teased, putting his arm around her.

"Yes, for some of it."

"What do you mean?"

"Oh, you know, there are people who only feel alive when they cause commotion. But apparently it didn't serve Jacquelyn because she abruptly left again, and this time she missed out on something special."

"What was it?"

"Well, let's say she might have found a constructive outlet for her theatrics. One of the guests was a producer seeking performers for his winter production."

"Too bad—she could use an outlet," Thad smirked.

"And I watched another woman also leave in a fit, but you don't know her, so I'll spare the details. I just wonder what it will take for them to change," Amelia mused.

"They'll probably change when they want to."

His profound words were simple, yet so true. The wisdom gave Amelia peace. She felt off kilter since their only son, Ivan, started college the same year as the death of her parents. Had it not been for something spectacular occurring, she might have become unglued over the series of losses in her life.

Thad left the room to prepare dinner. Amelia filled his spot on the couch with a generous pillow and snuggled against it. She closed her eyes, remembering her life-changing moment.

One summer day, the gardener pointed to a large, iridescent blue dragonfly hovering over the hood of her car. She watched the beautiful insect circle the shiny surface as though it was a pool of water. And then it happened—Amelia fell into the in-between-space—the great unknown no one can explain.

She put her hand out and said, "Come here."

To her surprise, the dragonfly flew directly onto her palm and rested there. She stood in suspended reality, feeling the winged creature's consciousness unifying with her own. Amelia was deluged with a powerful stream of Universal Love. It gave her the very feeling of hopefulness she needed at the time.

The dragonfly had complete trust in her through a mysterious, intertwined energy of their thoughts. She extended her hand over the car's shimmering surface. Once again, it circled the hood's reflected light. Amelia looked at the gardener, who stood in awe. There was nothing to be said.

In her mind and in her life, Amelia was slowly shifting her perception of truth. She recalled the past August when she had been lured to the Victorian's musty attic. Under the ghost's influence, she followed him into the turret. She sat on a round stone in the center, realizing it was a place unlike the world she just left. The room filled with exquisite sounds of the cosmos and celestial music of spinning spheres.

A full-length mirror lit up in three-dimensional images. Earth appeared as a peaceful, living, breathing planet, emerging from the vastness of space. Continents and oceans, rain forests, deserts, mountain ranges, waterfalls, deep crystal caves, plains and lush forests, creatures large and small were being shown to Amelia. She saw land masses connected by undersea canyons, interlocking waterways and channels, as well as the flourishing of ocean life.

The kaleidoscope of earth's splendor and bounty grew dimmer, as she sadly witnessed the toll of human pollution and the unwise use of natural resources—like a plague on the fragile environment. The images in the mirror evaporated.

The ghost, as though behind a watery shield, spoke something she never before considered. "Amelia, you must become a teacher and preserve what came before."

Thad interrupted his wife's reverie, entering the room with a plate of food. "There's more to Daphne's school than you ever shared, isn't there?" he asked as he sat down.

"I wish you knew," Amelia sighed, beginning to connect the dots in her life. "I have an idea."

"What is it?" Thad braced himself, hoping her idea would not usurp one of his own he wanted to suggest.

"I love Franklin Port for its clean harbor and beaches. I'd like us to buy an old, waterfront house I accidentally passed when I made a wrong turn. It could be a business— a Bed and Breakfast we can run together—if you wanted to." Amelia's voice trailed off, knowing he'd probably reject her proposal.

"Really? Are you kidding?" Thad sat forward and looked her squarely in the eyes.

"No, I'm dead serious. And…it has another building right on the beach, a school, where I can teach and create a conservation center for protecting the wetlands." Amelia realized she could not save the earth, but she could save a precious part of it. It was as if the ghost's words became her own passionate mission, where she had none before.

Amelia recognized everything in her life was flawlessly planned— having been in science, her sadness which brought her to Daphne's school, and passing the property—as if part of a cosmic labyrinth. It all hinged upon Thad's response. He was twiddling his thumbs like he did when tolerating one of her brainstorms. One could only hear the crackling fire.

Amelia was certain Thad was about to dismiss her plan with one of his long-winded rationalizations as to why it was not a good idea. Now she braced herself.

"It appears nothing is by chance. I know the buildings you're talking about. I took a wrong turn recently and ended up in the same place. The property caught my eye, too. I imagined it being restored. Let's do it — we can use a change of direction."

Amelia was so stunned she found herself opposing him. "The buildings could be too expensive to restore," she voiced.

"Yes, but we have the bonus I told you about at dinner after what's-her-name left the Port Empress."

Amelia kissed his cheek, amazed by the fortuitous timing of the money. "What are the odds of this happening, and what's gotten into you, Thad, that you're so agreeable?" Amelia laughed, not expecting an answer.

A multitude of phenomena had to come together for her and Thad to be able to act upon an opportunity of a lifetime — and it did not escape Amelia's appreciation. Coincidence, an unseen force at work, is not by chance as people think it to be.

CHAPTER 16

The Beggar

ONCE THE FRANKLIN Port Theater was refurbished to an up-scale, fully equipped venue, its proximity to the city attracted aspiring talent looking to break into show business. The proud board invited renowned producer, Miles Goode, for its first stage show.

Circulars announcing an audition date for Goode's winter musical, Victorian Times in London, were delivered to local residents. Competition was stiff. More than eighty people showed up for fewer than twenty parts. None could have anticipated the odd way Miles planned to choose his actors.

"Your audition will be portraying characters on the streets during the Franklin Port house tour. The most convincing actors during the event will perform on stage in January. If you need costumes, help yourselves to the period clothing I brought with me," he said, motioning to overflowing bins and racks.

The house tour was the biggest draw among the town's holiday festivities and designed to raise money for a local charity. This year, the Franklin Port Pantry was unanimously voted recipient of ticket proceeds. In addition, a can of food was required for admission. Daphne agreed to put her Victorian on the circuit at Cassandra's request. The event sold double the usual number of tickets to curious townspeople, all hoping to confirm intriguing stories heard over the years.

§ § §

Preparing for the tour, the festival committee began decorating shortly after Thanksgiving. Being allowed inside the Victorian for the first time, the ladies felt overpowered by the dramatically high ceilings and heavy moldings exaggerating them further. The biddies couldn't avoid being loose-lipped.

"Do you think Daphne lives here by herself?" Mildred asked the others in a hushed voice.

"Oh, she's not alone all the time, mark my words," Hedy proclaimed.

"I see a man leaving late at night—it goes on all the time. I get a good view from my house down the street," she said smugly while trimming the Christmas tree. "And binoculars do help," she admitted.

"Really?" Mildred stood with her hands on her wide hips. The gossip was getting good. "Just who is he?"

"Charles Hinds," Hedy gushed. "You know—the owner of the Port Empress Inn."

The women gasped in astonishment. Charles was the most well-liked and eligible bachelor in town. Female hearts of all ages went pitter-patter whenever he walked into a room. How many of those staid, older ladies would drop in their tracks if he were to cast one of his smiles their way? This news was both an enviable situation and a curiosity. No one could quite get a grasp on the elusive, oddball owner of the very house they were decorating.

"Why would Mr. Hinds be visiting Daphne? Isn't she supposed to be married?" Mildred asked.

"All I can say is this place is steeped in scandal from way back," Hedy answered.

Stoked by rumors, each woman added her own fantastic tale about the friction between the Victorian's original owner, Dr. Arthur Wake, and his brother, Simon. Hedy mentioned the scuttlebutt about an inheritance with huge sums of money, stolen by Simon. Supposedly, the discord contributed to the death of Arthur's bride and plunged Arthur into the depths of sadness. The more the women blabbered, the harder their task seemed. Their arms felt heavy while working on the twelve-foot fir tree by the front windows.

When the untimely death of Simon was mentioned, the atmosphere in the room changed. The temperature dropped, and Hedy complained of circulation problems. Knocking sounds from inside the walls alarmed them enough to stop talking about the Wake family. They quickly finished decorating the tree.

Once completed, the women stepped back to get a final look before leaving. Regrettably, they waited a minute too long. Lights strung over the branches began flickering. The ladies stood with coats half on, gaping. What they saw was beyond anything natural. The tree began swaying, dislodging ornaments and shedding needles, as if it hadn't been properly secured in its stand.

Hedy bravely went over to steady it when the tree levitated and floated to the center of the room. The electric lights became unplugged in the process—but they remained lit. En masse, the screaming women ran out the door and directly to town hall.

"It's far too dangerous in Betel's Victorian!" Hedy shrieked the minute she barged into the mayor's office. "I specifically told you not to put her house on our tour."

"Calm down…calm down," the mayor said, dismissing everyone's hysteria.

"The place is overrun with spirits. They nearly scared me to death," Mildred exclaimed, clutching at her heart.

"Yes…yes…things float…and walls knock. Believe me, it's haunted," another woman chimed in.

Hearing the uproar, office workers gathered outside the mayor's office. Some agreed the Victorian could be a problem for the town's reputation. It was already a bigger-than-life presence in the village. Many people crossed the street to avoid walking past it—afraid of something rubbing off. However, the money generated from ticket sales became the deciding factor, and the mayor refused to change his mind.

As the women continued to jabber, the mayor laughed, rejecting their protests as nonsense. Ticket sales skyrocketed. In Franklin Port, a good story could spread faster than wildfire.

§ § §

When the long-awaited day arrived, mounting expectation was in the air. Aspiring actors in full costume dispersed throughout the village according to characters Miles assigned them. They were given roles in contrast to their personas. Successful businessmen were dressed as chimney sweeps, and some of the less stylish women were the grand dames in velvet, wide-brimmed hats with woolen muffs. Beggars and street urchins wore threadbare clothing, the most uncomfortable assignments in cold weather. If you wanted to be on stage for the upcoming production, you were grateful for any part. The lead role was a lady-of-the-night. It would be given to some lucky woman who could also sing like an angel.

Daphne planned to hold her final class for the year during the evening house tour. To stay out of the way, she set up the round room on the tower's second floor. The curved windows were lit with electric candles. Fresh greenery, held in place by red velvet ribbons, cascaded across the sills.

Once the students arrived, Daphne passed around her dish of chocolates. "Take one to seal your intention for the coming New Year," she instructed. "Remember, I'm going away for a few weeks, and tonight will be our last scheduled class." Watching them carefully pick their chocolate, savor it, and then set a goal, she asked, "Has anyone's dream come true?"

"Mine's coming true," Amelia volunteered. "A lot of seemingly unrelated events recently converged, and my life has taken on a different direction."

"Synchronicity," Daphne responded.

"I'm so sorry to interrupt," Gwen said, squinting and rubbing her eyes. "There's a woman outside in dire straits. She's wearing a tattered, dirty coat and begging for food. We should help her."

Cassandra was the first to look out the window.

"Gwen," Daphne calmly said. "Actors are auditioning for the winter theater performance. The beggars have to collect everyone's food donations for the pantry."

"That's clever," Cassandra nodded.

Gwen was convinced the woman was not an actor, but a real beggar. Her conviction brought the others to the windows. Daphne dimmed the overhead chandelier so they could have a better look outside. Their faces were pressed against the glass. It was a spectacle to the hundred or more people lining Main Street, awaiting a chance to get inside the notorious Victorian.

A stooped, shivering woman was begging for food. She seemed truly in need, as Gwen had said. Eager to help, the students raced down the staircase and through the front doors, pushing aside folks on the tour. The indigent woman took off faster than any person in that condition could ever run—a most peculiar inconsistency. Even youthful Cassandra wasn't able to catch up with her.

What a sight—Daphne's students following after some poor, unfortunate beggar. People on the tour line were thrilled something must surely be afoot in the rambling house and didn't mind the hour-long wait. A glimpse of a ghost seemed guaranteed and well worth the ticket price.

§ § §

"What did you make of that?" the students asked each other, returning to the second floor.

"The woman was acting, and she's someone we know," Daphne said.

"Let me guess—Jacquelyn?" Amelia questioned.

"Exactly."

Everyone roared with laughter. Cassandra had to hold her hands over her mouth to resist being the loudest. Daphne suggested they be respectful. "What goes around comes around. Choose wisely how you respond."

"Jacquelyn is so damn good at acting, she fooled the best of us," Amelia forced herself to acknowledge. "And maybe she has an obnoxious personality because she did miss her calling as an actress. One might say she is impoverished, if she's so far from her dream."

Cassandra wished she could gloat over the twist of fate at Jacquelyn's assignment. She joined the others at the windows to take another look. Jacquelyn returned to the line of people and continued begging. "If nothing else, Jacquelyn is persistent," Cassandra conceded. "She's doing something for a greater good, even if it's self-serving."

Jacquelyn looked up at the women watching her again. She was feeling terribly vulnerable, but instead of laughing at her, the students applauded.

CHAPTER 17

The Blizzard

THE WEEKEND FOLLOWING the house tour, Daphne phoned Sophia regarding their holiday at the Mount Hope Lodge, five hours north of Franklin Port. Sophia never balked at meeting her there, knowing the trip was based on another of Daphne's premonitions about Jason's father.

Charles stopped by the Victorian the evening before Daphne planned to leave. He sat at the kitchen table with a cup of coffee and listened to her itinerary, pondering how to interject his opinion on the matter. "I've made a decision. I refuse to let you go," he emphatically said.

Daphne gave him one of her classic looks. "I'm going. It's settled."

"It's an unreasonable time of year to travel north by yourself," he argued. "I've been on the mountain road in winter—it's treacherous. Postpone it until after the holidays when things are slower at the Inn, and I can join you." Charles was grappling with some inner radar he felt to keep Daphne safe.

"I can't postpone it."

"Why...what's so important that it can't be delayed? Are you meeting a man?" Charles had only a platonic relationship with Daphne and hoped it would become more serious, but suppressed his desires until he was sure she might want the same. Now he had a hunch there could be somebody else in her life he didn't know about.

"Another man...hmm, sounds interesting," Daphne teased.

Charles pretended to be unbothered by her response. "Why don't you travel south?" he proposed.

"You don't understand—I have to go. I'm leaving first thing in the morning. I'll call you when I arrive safe and sound," she promised, smiling at his kindhearted concern.

As she walked him to the back door, he wheeled around and grabbed her firmly by the arm. "No, you mustn't go alone. I'll need some time to make the necessary arrangements to close the Inn so I can go with you."

"I can't ask you to do that."

"It's done, my pretty lady. You have no choice in the matter. I'll be here late morning to pick you up."

"You're wasting your energy, Charles. I'll be gone by then."

His grip tightened. "You won't be gone. Be ready at noon." Charles left, having no idea how he allowed his holiday business to be thrown into the ringer, but reasoned the Inn needed a few upgrades, and this presented a perfect time to start the job.

§ § §

Daphne went to her bedroom to pack. Stunned by his assertiveness, she was glad Charles didn't press for the real reason she was going. He would think it absurd if he knew she was chasing after an unknown man who fathered Jason. She folded her warm flannel pajamas and placed them in a suitcase, and then opened a dresser drawer for a few other items. Lying on top was the silk nightgown she wore while dancing with Arthur in the parlor. "Boy, those days are gone," she said nostalgically. Her heart skipped a beat at the fanciful idea of being intimate with Charles. She considered taking it along just in case, but the drawer slammed shut. She pulled it open again, thinking it had closed from the dip in the floor. A second time, the drawer closed before she could remove any of the fine lingerie. She finished packing only what was practical and went to bed.

§ § §

A hint of cinnamon permeated the house. Half awake, Daphne looked at the clock, 5 AM. She returned to a light sleep with dreams of preparing French toast for her children when they were young. The aroma grew stronger. Daphne sat up. "Who's cooking breakfast?" she called out.

The house was dark. She got out of bed and put on a robe, thinking Charles must have let himself in. Halfway down the staircase, she could hear sounds in the kitchen—butter sizzling.

"Charles?"

There was no answer.

"Charles, why are you here so early?" she asked from the vestibule.

There still was no answer.

"Charles!" she called out even louder, suspecting someone hiding in the shadows.

Daphne stopped in the kitchen doorway. A small, burning candle on the table gave off dancing light, enough for her to see a single place setting. The gas was on under the frying pan, and a thick slice of sugar-coated bread was browning in melted butter.

"Where are you?" she whispered. A knot was forming in her stomach.

A man's arm grabbed her from behind and pulled her by the waist. She tried getting away, but his other arm went around her chest and held her tightly against himself.

"Charles, stop! What are you doing?" Daphne was not at all pleased with his little game. She struggled to escape.

"Shh...I'm here."

Her body went limp, and she was breathless. "Arthur..."

The ghost had never completely materialized to solid human form before. No longer transparent, he was holding her—wanting her. Daphne turned to see his face. His eyes penetrated to the depths of her soul—unleashing a distant memory of him.

He untied the belt of her robe and let it fall to the floor, then ran his hands down her arms. Soft light followed his touch. She begged him for more, but he vanished as always before, leaving her sobbing inconsolably.

The bread began burning. Daphne reluctantly came to her senses. Turning off the gas, she lifted the toast to the plate and sat down to eat. In front of her, she could see a message scrawled in spilled sugar on the table's surface: You're mine.

§ § §

Charles was on time, exactly noon. "You look gorgeous," he said, stuffing her luggage into the trunk. "I'm not used to seeing you wearing makeup."

Daphne beamed from his compliment, realizing it had been a long time since she bothered to fuss over herself. Sitting between them was a wicker basket. "What's this?" she asked.

"The chef packed us snacks for the journey."

Charles looked over at her, wanting to hold her hand, before placing both his hands on the steering wheel and driving off.

Unusually quiet for most of the trip, Daphne was lost in thought, not about Charles, but of escapades she conjured in her mind—wild, impassioned musings brought on by the various men in her life.

There was Charles who loved her, a husband who remained at a distance, and a ghost who enchained her heart. It was difficult for Daphne to reconcile her earthly needs with Arthur's enduring power. She lived in two worlds, and only had a scant notion of why, which she tried resolving by writing fantasies and wisdom in her diaries.

"A penny for your thoughts," Charles spoke, wanting conversation.

Daphne glanced his way, aware she caved into his wish to accompany her. She liked his forcefulness the night before, but now he was more his usual self—reserved—resigned to an indefinable barrier between them.

"Huh? Did the cat get your tongue?" he asked, perplexed by her ability to maintain such an air of solitude while being with him.

She reached across the seat to rub the back of his neck. Feeling more open, Daphne revealed the purpose of her trip to the mountain, every detail.

"That's such a long shot, Daphne," Charles groaned. "So many years have passed since Jason was born. What are you going on when you don't even have a name?"

"It's a feeling in my bones."

"Well, I hope it's worth the effort."

"Once we get there, we'll enjoy ourselves—trust me—and you'll get to meet Sophia."

Charles bit his tongue.

Daphne was glad not to be traveling alone. She began to look upon Charles differently. Perhaps he was her knight in shining armor. Maybe love went beyond the intense experience she was seeking to something less fiery—simple kindness.

§ § §

Just as the sun was setting, Charles and Daphne stopped at the foot of the mountain for dinner. They needed sustenance before traveling the infamously grueling road leading to the lodge. Lingering over coffee and dessert, they laughed and enjoyed each other's company.

Once back in the car, Daphne noticed the manager of the eatery turning the door sign around to read CLOSED, shutting off all the lights, and locking up as he exited. She thought it odd, considering she could still see a man inside standing at a window—the same one who continuously stared at her during dinner. That didn't bother Charles as much as the manager's parting words to him, warning of a blizzard heading their way. The weather forecast predicted absolutely no snow. They drove up the mountain, each pondering something different.

The brisk mountain air was dramatically colder. After an hour of driving, lights strung along ski lifts became visible. Daphne moved the empty basket between them to the back seat, grabbed a blanket, and curled up next to Charles with girl-like excitement as they drew closer to Mount Hope Lodge. A silver moon, appearing only yards away the higher they went, illuminated the narrow road. The weather could not have been clearer. Charles wondered what on earth the manager meant. Since he didn't heed his words at the bottom, it didn't make sense to remain uneasy so close to the summit.

In an instant, full darkness descended upon the mountain, wrapped in a frozen cloud. It was a surprise attack of Nature pouncing upon the unsuspecting. The twinkling lights were no longer visible. At once, heavy snow fell. Their vehicle skidded on ice, leaving the rear end partially hanging off the edge of the road, teetering over a ravine that greedily sucked up huge flakes, filling its deep cavern. Charles panicked at the thought of sliding off the cliff.

Approaching headlights barely penetrated their snow-covered windows. Neither he nor Daphne had any visibility. Charles tried opening his door to flag down help, but it wouldn't budge — the snow was already too deep. He heard a rhythmic clanking of tire chains coming closer and held his breath, thinking another car might make the situation worse if the driver didn't see them. Why, he tried to imagine, would Daphne take this dangerous trip chasing after some vague notion? Hiding immense fear, Charles looked at her. She remained unshaken.

A metallic clink sounded from his front bumper. He believed the slightest movement would send them plunging down the blanketed gorge, not to be found until spring. With one wrenching tug forward, they were pulled onto the road and towed up the mountain by something they couldn't see.

Shortly afterwards, they were unhitched and left to drive on their own again. Charles looked to Daphne for an explanation, but in his heart, he knew it came from the other world where she dwelled at times.

§ § §

Mount Hope Lodge looked spectacular beneath the clear, star-filled sky. Skiers were coming in for the night after taking their last run before the lifts closed. They made a long procession carrying lit torches rather than poles, marking the beginning of holiday festivities. A valet opened their doors. Daphne looked around, filled with enthusiasm and hope.

"What about the blizzard?" Charles asked the young man dressed in a royal blue uniform.

"What blizzard, sir?"

"We were just in a horrible blizzard. Look, my car is piled with snow." Charles went silent. His car was dry.

"No, sir, it hasn't snowed for three weeks, and none is in the forecast. Enjoy your stay at Mount Hope Lodge."

Monday, December 15

I hear the rustling of leaves beneath the pounding hooves of a stallion. The knight is charging toward my castle on his mighty steed. He suddenly stops, his eyes feasting upon me. Captivated by my beauty, he lifts me, a powerful priestess, up to the saddle. We gallop out the castle gates into the mists of time. The wind whistles through my flowing hair. ~D~

CHAPTER 18

Mount Hope Lodge

DAPHNE AND CHARLES entered the welcoming doors of Mount Hope Lodge onto rugs so plush their footsteps were but a whisper. Christmas was approaching and decorations reflected a bountiful ambiance. Greenery, entwined with gold ribbons, was festooned around and up the staircase banisters. Brilliant poinsettias graced the lobby, giving one a dash of nostalgia for the simplicity of past eras—a rare resort dripping in old world luxury. The colossal fireplace burned brightly. Its intensity drew in pungent whiffs of pine needles from regal trees claiming the surrounding mountainside.

The lodge was imbued with European flavor after a corporation called AJ Mountain Resorts bought the original cabins some thirty years before. It developed the mountain's summit into a town replete with restaurants, shops, and even a constabulary for the quarrelsome few who lingered too long in the bars. The lodge remained popular with the wealthy as their getaway playground, yet was surprisingly affordable for the less affluent—an unexpected combination.

While Charles registered, Daphne heard her name called by a white-gloved concierge, dressed in a woolen uniform ribbed with red around the neck and cuffs. "Daphne Betel—telegram. Daphne Betel—telegram."

Walking to the man, she lifted a small note off the silver tray he held. Daphne anticipated news about her daughter's travel plans from Europe. This was to be their first reunion in several years, and she couldn't wait. Her heart sank upon reading the telegram.

Mom
Sorry not meeting you
Dad still here since Thanksgiving
All flying to Vienna for Mary's concert
Wish you would take plane and join us
Nancy

Nothing rattled Daphne more than the tug of family. She had second thoughts being at the lodge when her loved ones were on the other side of the world, celebrating together.

"Daphne, Daphne," Sophia Wells called, rushing across the opulent lobby. In her exuberance, she nearly tripped over someone's luggage. "Daphne, I'm so happy to see you again," she said, yanking off her woolen ski cap and releasing a mop of soft, light-brown curls. Sophia's long eyelashes accentuated big brown eyes. Years working as a night-shift nurse in a city hospital kept her slim and agile. She couldn't wait to hit the slopes with her best friend, like in the old days.

"Sophia, look at you — you're still so beautiful. Your smile makes you more so. I only wish I were in higher spirits right now." Daphne and Sophia hugged each other after a long lapse of time since they had been together.

"What's wrong?" Sophia questioned.

Daphne handed her the telegram.

"Oh…I feel bad. Here you are trying to help me find Jason's father, and you're missing out. You've always dreamed of being with your family for the holidays."

"Don't be silly, Soph, you know I'm terrified of the sea and won't fly across the ocean."

Room keys in hand, Charles caught up with the women, wondering why Daphne appeared so sullen. She showed him the telegram. A part of him was relieved things would be simpler without Daphne's daughter.

"Forgive my manners. Sophia, this is my friend, Charles."

Charles flinched at being referred to as merely a friend. He politely shook Sophia's hand, although he secretly wished the trip didn't include anyone besides Daphne, or never happened at all. Not knowing how to address the telegram, he excused himself to admire the lobby's period furnishings, while the women chatted.

"I feel lucky this time," Daphne assured Sophia, changing the topic from the telegram. "I know there's a clue about Jason's father up here, but if not, it might be my last hurrah trying. Whatever the outcome, at least we'll still have our friendship, won't we?" she asked, concerned.

"Of course we will. At this point, I wouldn't know what to do if we did find him." Sophia laughed, watching Charles on the other side of the room. "But forget about Jason's father. Is this the man you're always talking about?"

"Not really."

"Oh…then why did you invite him along?"

"He invited himself."

Charles returned to the ladies with a bellhop to escort them to their three separate rooms, four floors up.

In Daphne's suite, alone for the first time all day, she chomped down on a tiny piece of wrapped chocolate left on the pillow. Had she been less glum, she might have noticed it tasted exactly the same as her own chocolates. More importantly, she was oblivious to the circle image on top.

After freshening up, the three met again for a nightcap in the dining hall. Daphne did not see the buffet table's carved details, identical to those of her own table she purchased from the Wake estate. One can only wonder what she would have thought had she been more observant of the Invisible world stirring.

They went to bed early. In the middle of the night, Daphne had a frightening dream. Someone called out, "Impending danger! Impending danger!" She awoke, fretting. Daphne often had prophetic dreams, but they were more specific—who was in danger? Terrified of falling asleep again, she turned on a lamp and read until the sun rose.

Early morning, Charles knocked on Daphne's door, hurrying her to eat before skiing. Daphne put the nightmare out of her mind, dressed, and met Charles and Sophia for breakfast. Ski conditions were perfect. An unexpected storm in the middle of the night had dropped twenty-five inches of fresh snow in less than an hour—a blizzard, they were informed.

CHAPTER 19

Ghostly Brewings

J ACQUELYN DAYE LANDED the lead part, lady-of-the-night, in Miles Goode's musical production. The solos were tailor-made to show off her beautiful voice. With a bit of uncharacteristic generosity, she decided to give Daphne several complimentary tickets to the performances. Jacquelyn arrived at the Victorian. From the street, it appeared to be in darkness. "Another one of Daphne's absurd classes," she scoffed.

She pulled into the Victorian's driveway leading to the rear. Only one small light by the back entrance was on. Jacquelyn hesitated. The car's headlights illuminated a foreboding sight. Bending, snow-covered boughs of towering pines appeared as threatening arms of giants. The eeriness would have been enough for her to leave immediately, but a note taped to the door caught her attention. Jacquelyn stepped from her car to read it: School closed until January 30th. Disappointed, she put the tickets under the mat.

Turning to leave, the car door slammed shut in front of her. "Wind," she reasoned, nervously tugging at the door's handle. A shadowy figure ran across the porch and into the vastness of the Victorian's yard. Hands trembling, Jacquelyn jumped behind the wheel. Milky-colored balls of light began darting off the shrubbery and roof, acting as a sentinel army guarding the property. "Stop it! I know better than to believe all those contrived stories about the house being haunted. Daphne makes them up just to generate business," she vented.

Jacquelyn drove off, swerving to avoid the circles of light, lest they get angry and follow. Her heart was pounding with fear. "I can't stand Daphne's house and those people. Whatever was I thinking inviting any of them to the theatre? I need a drink." She pulled up to the Port Empress Inn and saw it, too, was unexpectedly dark. Slowing down, Jacquelyn could read a sign posted out front: Inn closed until January 30th. Her blood started to boil over the possibility Daphne and Charles were vacationing together.

Jacquelyn parked her car and walked up the front steps, hoping an employee might give her more information. Something started nibbling

95

her ear. It poked her back, making her spin full circle. No one was there. She smelled a nauseating stench of stale beer, as though someone was breathing in front of her. "Who's here?"

Footprints formed next to hers on the snowy porch. Another set appeared, even larger, alongside the first. Jacquelyn felt weak, blood draining from her head. A crushing pressure against her back pushed her toward the door. She desperately banged on it for help, but to no avail. Fear overtook her, and she fainted into a heap.

§ § §

Charles Hinds hired Jason to renovate the Inn's main floor while he was away with Daphne. Jason returned that night to be certain he locked up and was shocked to find a woman lying on the porch, half frozen and barely breathing. He recognized it was Jacquelyn from Daphne's party and carried her inside to the velvet couch in the lobby. While putting his lips against hers to force in his warm breath, she stirred.

Jason found several coverlets to wrap around her shivering body before racing to the reception desk to phone for help. There was no dial tone. He hurriedly lit wood in the fireplace for warmth and light, and returned to the couch to rub her freezing hands.

Now fully alert, she pulled her hands away. "What are you doing?"

"I found you lying outside. A few minutes longer and you might have died," he explained.

"How did we get in here?" Jacquelyn looked around and recognized the Port Empress Inn.

"I have a key. Charles asked me to do work while he's on vacation."

"Where did Charles go?" Jacquelyn sounded like an edgy, jealous wife.

Jason was offended by the barrage of questions. He moved away, ignoring them. Jacquelyn readjusted her rumpled clothing while Jason stood next to the fireplace, one arm resting on the mantle, staring at her.

"Do you believe in…ghosts?" she sweetly asked.

He hesitated to answer, confused by the sudden sincerity in her voice. "Yes, I was taught about spirits as a child."

"What? Is everyone in this hick town insane like Daphne and those nutty students?"

"That's enough!" Jason's voice echoed off the wooden walls, sounding more like ten men in unison. "Come over here," he demanded.

Held under a spell, Jacquelyn rose from the couch. She glided to the fireplace with toes pointing downward, as though two strong-armed men were carrying a wench to their captain. An unseen presence of bawdy drunkards on barstools taunted her with vulgar cheers. Loud voices and sounds of thick beer mugs thumping on the bar came out of thin air. Jacquelyn was now treading upon the mysterious space Amelia spoke about. In a muddled state of mind, she saw an opportunity to be with Jason after all. Their eyes met—the night was hers to use.

"Come closer," Jason said with bravado, feeling bewitched. He drew her head back to kiss her neck, inhaling a scent of sweet musk. "Take off your cardigan," he ordered.

She began unbuttoning. When she reached the last two, he ran his fingers across her satiny skin, took hold of the sweater, and in a swift pull, ripped both sides apart. Only the ping of buttons landing on the stone hearth could be heard. Holding Jacquelyn's shoulders, Jason moved her against the paneled wall.

The spirits fully awakened. The room became as a rocking ship in a storm, thrashing the couple about. Its movement breached their embrace, giving Jacquelyn moments of feigned escape. But there was no escape— only the game of cat and mouse around the walls in the spellbound heat of their passion.

Just as they were about to fall onto the couch in mindless ecstasy, Jason backed up against a wall panel, causing it to pop open. The torrid moment was lost. Not wanting Jacquelyn to see the opening, he realized he had to get rid of her. Jason walked across the room, scooped up her belongings, and led her to the door.

"What the hell are you doing?" she protested.

Jason was too preoccupied with the secret compartment to answer. He briskly escorted Jacquelyn outside with her clothing thrown over her shoulders, mumbling disjointed words about doing the honorable thing. He went back inside. Hearing him lock the Inn's door, she stumbled to her car in the freezing night, half dressed.

"I'll get even with you for this, you can bet on it!" she shouted with indignation. Wheels spinning on the slick road, Jacquelyn made her way home. She drank a glass of wine, curled up on the couch under blankets, and tried to pretend nothing unusual happened.

Jason, however, couldn't wait to investigate the hole in the wall. He took a deep breath, put his hand inside, and pulled out a dusty portfolio with a brass lock. Its aged leather made the embossed name almost imperceptible—Dr. Arthur Wake.

He reached in again, eagerly searching for a key, but there was none. Instead, he found an unstamped envelope yellowed by time, held closed with sealing wax, also addressed to Dr. Arthur Wake. Jason slipped it safely under the portfolio's flap and put the intriguing find into his briefcase.

When he locked the front door for the night, he felt a slap on his back. The wind whispered in his ear, "Good job."

CHAPTER 20

Open Portal

J ASON RESTORED MANY historic buildings over the years and encountered strange situations which he often attributed to ghosts. He was now convinced the Port Empress Inn was haunted after what happened between him and Jacquelyn. His booming voice and the room's rocking motions were not normal. While he was certainly attracted to her, under ordinary circumstances he would never behave in such a way.

Jason returned to Daphne's Victorian where he was staying during her vacation. He removed the portfolio from his briefcase and placed it on the dining table, wanting to break its lock with his hammer. As he lifted the tool to smash it, his wrist twisted, and the hammer dropped to the floor. He reached for the sealed envelope under the flap, but it flew across the room and also landed on the floor.

"Oh crap!" he exclaimed, picking up the letter to slip back into place.

Jason stared at the portfolio, imagining what secrets it might hold. Maybe there were valuables inside. It was oh so tempting to open, but he was afraid to try a second time, not wanting to match wits with a ghost. He poured a glass of scotch and entered the parlor to mull over the bizarre night, deciding to call Jacquelyn and apologize. "I'll say I had too much to drink. No, no, that would not even begin to cover it. Well, I'll think of something." He found Daphne's personal phone book and went page by page until he saw Jacquelyn written in the margin. "I'll bet it's her." He dialed.

"Hello," a drowsy voice answered.

"Jacquelyn, this is Jason and I'm calling to..."

She slammed down the phone. His response was to top off his scotch and stretch out on the apple-green couch. The stiff drink soon put him into a deep sleep.

The room suddenly got colder. "Get out," a man shouted. Jason jumped to his feet before he was fully awake. His heart was racing—he didn't see anyone. "Come back when you're sober," the voice insisted.

Jason thought someone was talking to him.

"I hate you and I'm never coming back," a drunken, younger voice responded.

Scared out of his mind, Jason looked around again and was shocked when two transparent, spectral figures formed before his eyes. One was a tall, scowling, dark-haired man, while a younger man had his hand on the doorknob to leave. The apparitions faded. Shaking in disbelief, Jason was jolted once more when the phone rang.

"Jason, is everything okay?" Daphne asked from her suite at the lodge. The odd timing of her call unnerved him.

"Yes, yes, the house is fine." He struggled for composure. "But I was working at the Port Empress Inn. Uh…it's a long story. I found some stuff I think you should see and…well…these things are old," Jason stammered.

"You know they belong to Charles," Daphne argued.

"No, no, you need to have them. There's a portfolio and a sealed envelope—both with Dr. Arthur Wake's name on the outside."

Daphne, warming herself by a blazing fire in her suite, felt a hair-raising chill, fully engaging her sixth sense. She had the dire need to get hold of the items as soon as possible, no longer considering Charles.

"Jason, it can't wait until I return home. I know you're too busy to travel, but Amelia and Gwen are coming here after the New Year. Please ask them to bring what you found."

"I will. I'm seeing Amelia and her husband tomorrow morning to give them blueprints for their Bed and Breakfast." Jason said goodbye and slumped back down on the couch. He finished his scotch and drifted into another sound sleep.

§ § §

There was no sun the next day. Gray snow clouds hung overhead. Jason reoriented himself and changed clothes to make his appointment with the Fultons at the wetlands property. He rolled up their renovation plans and left with them under his arm.

Amelia approached Jason as soon as he arrived. "Hi, Jason, you look exhausted. Is everything okay?"

"Yeah, the usual," he responded. "Daphne said you and Gwen are meeting her at the lodge. Will you take something with you to give her?"

"Okay. We're going January 2nd. Do you have it with you now?"

"No," he answered, hitting his forehead in exasperation for being absent-minded. "We have more than a week. I'll get it to you before you go. Here are the blueprints I promised your husband. You can call me tonight to discuss the details."

Jason headed to the Port Empress Inn to work. Three black, Model T police cars from another era were parked in front with officers standing on the porch. On the verge of panicking, Jason got out of his truck and put his shaking hands in his jacket pockets. "What's going on, officer?"

"A woman died here last night," the policeman told him.

Jason was aghast.

"She was pregnant," another one added. "Probably couldn't get medical help in time and bled to death giving birth."

Jason's mind swirled, recalling Jacquelyn lying on the exact spot. He supported himself against the railing, trying to figure out which incident was reality—the tragedy this officer was describing or his own encounter last night with Jacquelyn. He called her and was certain he heard her voice, so he knew she couldn't have died.

The first policeman pointed to bloody hand prints as well as a pool of frozen blood on the planking. "It looks like she was pounding on the door to get inside."

Jason feared he was being suspected of a crime. "What about the baby?" he asked, realizing they said only the woman died.

"The infant survived and was taken to its father, Dr. Arthur Wake."

Dr. Wake was long dead, and Jason knew nothing about him having children. His knees buckled, and he squeezed his eyes shut. When he opened them, the officers were gone, the police cars disappeared, and the bloodstains vanished. Delirious, Jason entered the Inn and went right to where he remembered the secret compartment. That certainly was real, he thought. He purposely left the panel ajar for when he returned, but now it was closed.

The walls were lined in individual squares of exquisite wood. Jason forgot which square opened during his escapade with Jacquelyn. After trying several places, he began frantically pushing and banging everywhere, but nothing budged. Jason took his pry bar and in a fit ripped off all the paneling. He was desperate to find the hidden chamber and prove to himself he had not gone mad.

An hour later there was a filthy mess. Jason felt numb as he viewed a once stately room, now in shambles. "What have I done? Why did I do this?" In the heap of woodwork on the floor was an old photograph. Jason shook it to remove the debris. He saw a beautiful young woman standing between two men. A deep sadness and a longing with no name overcame him. He slipped the photograph into his pocket to add to the portfolio and left the Inn for the day.

CHAPTER 21

Letting the Past Go

I T WAS THE morning of Christmas Eve. A twenty-five foot fir tree was carried into the sprawling lobby of Mount Hope Lodge by a group of brawny lumberjacks who hauled it along the old logging road. As every year prior, the resort's executive officer closed all the lobby's entryways while Santa's helpers secretly trimmed the giant tree and decorated the space.

Chefs fired up ovens and prepared out-of-this-world delicacies and endless trays of cookies and tempting desserts. Candy canes and chocolates were artfully arranged around bowls of eggnog, hot cider, and spiked punch. When the doors opened at 2 PM, guests were caught up by the magical scene.

A trio of musicians was tucked away in an alcove near the main sitting room, playing holiday songs. Some people sang to the pleasure of others who were relaxing in deep cushioned couches. No one ever knew who was behind the grand show, but many suspected only someone with a fanciful childhood could create such a joyous holiday atmosphere. It was rumored the anonymous organizer would weave through the crowd to witness everyone's enjoyment—and part of the fun was to figure out who it might be.

Daphne paid little attention to any of it. She hadn't slept since speaking to Jason. Her call to him was, ironically, just after another dream of impending danger. Jason's message about the portfolio and letter made her apprehensive, thinking they might be connected to her nightmare. It was as though her emotional stability had a little tear in it, inviting something vexing to seep in.

The music reminded Daphne of her daughter's concert in Vienna. But even if she didn't have a fear of the ocean, it would not be fair to Sophia and Charles to change plans last minute. They both made great sacrifices to be on Mount Hope for what seemed only another hunch. Daphne believed she was chasing after all the wrong things.

It was obvious how forlorn her friend looked when Sophia met her in the dining hall. "Daphne, after spending more than a week here and having nothing new revealed about Jason's father, let's just chalk this trip up as—we tried again."

"I guess so."

"I'm leaving tomorrow," Sophia said. "I'll visit Jason in Franklin Port for Christmas Day before heading back home. Enjoy the rest of your vacation with Charles— you know he adores you, don't you?"

Daphne looked at Sophia with empty eyes. Charles joined the women carrying beautifully wrapped gifts of scarves, gloves, and hats for each of them. It was the right opportunity for Daphne to give Charles a present, one she had long planned.

Considering the giver of the gift, he took his time opening the tiny package, wondering what unusual contents he might find. Expressionless, he held up a custom-made, gold money clip with a carved medallion of the historic ship, Port Empress. He embraced Daphne while giving the gift an awkward look. As much as he appreciated her thoughtfulness, the image wrenched him, but he had no idea why. His reaction escaped Daphne, as she had other thoughts on her mind.

Midnight—Christmas Day, 1969

I vow to stop searching for Jason's father. Perhaps it was just a convenient way for two friends to stay in touch, after all. If it is meant to be, then curious means will lead us to him. ~D~

CHAPTER 22

Wired

C HARLES WAS NEVER able to overcome the goings-on in Franklin Port, but at the lodge he still hoped to share some romantic time alone with Daphne. His only window of opportunity was after Sophia left and before a new shift of women arrived on the 2nd.

While dancing at a small bistro on the mountain, Charles lovingly held Daphne during slower melodies, hoping to dismantle her defenses. She invited him back to her suite for a nightcap. As she opened the cupboard for glasses, he grabbed her waist from behind and pulled her toward him. She tried getting away, but Charles put his other arm around her chest and held her tightly against himself.

"Charles, stop!" What are you doing?"

She turned around. Charles tried to ignite desire in her with his piercing blue eyes. He ran his hands down her arms. "You're mine," he whispered.

Startled, she abruptly pushed Charles away. Those were Arthur's words written in sugar the morning of the trip.

"Daphne, what's wrong?"

"Not this time," she answered with resignation—yearning for Arthur, instead.

Charles knew the night was not to be for lovers. He could only wish another chance with this woman might present itself.

§ § §

Amelia and Gwen left for Mount Hope as planned. They first stopped by the wetlands property where Jason and Thad were discussing renovations. Upon seeing Amelia, Jason rushed over with the package he wrapped in brown paper and tied with twine. Passing it through her car window, he insisted Amelia put it directly into Daphne's hands the moment she and Gwen arrive at the lodge. Amelia reached behind to place the parcel on the back seat.

"Would you please put it in the trunk?" Gwen requested.

"Is something wrong?"

"I don't know…that thing feels laden with strife."

Honoring Gwen's wishes, Amelia closed the trunk and they drove off, enjoying hours of conversation about many clandestine parts of their lives. Once reaching the foot of the mountain, like Daphne and Charles, they stopped for a light meal.

"Daphne has been here," Gwen divulged. "I'm sensing it."

"Probably so—this looks like the only place to eat before taking the mountain road."

The manager seated them in a booth and handed out menus. In no time, their order was served. About to take her last bite, Amelia noticed Gwen acting peculiar again. "What's wrong now?"

"The man sitting behind you has been staring out the window at your car throughout dinner," Gwen whispered with her hands cupped around her mouth. "You would think we have a dead body in the trunk."

Amelia turned her head to get a look, but there was no man in the booth or anyone else in the diner, except the manager. Concerned, she glanced out the window to be sure her car was still there. "It's kind of spooky you saw someone who isn't here. This trip is making me jumpy."

"Do you want to know the truth? I've been jumpy since you picked up the package from Jason," Gwen admitted.

The manager came over to them as they stood to leave. "Ladies, Are you traveling to Mount Hope Lodge?"

"Yes," Amelia answered. "Why do you ask?"

"A customer before you left his camera. Would you mind bringing it to the front desk?" The manager reached behind the counter for a new instant camera and several packs of film. "Here's the owner's name," he said, handing Gwen a piece of paper with scratchy handwriting.

The ladies paid their bill and walked to the door when the manager stopped them. "Wait a minute. It's not that I don't trust you, but I would like to take a snapshot of your license plate to keep a record of who has the camera."

Although thinking it odd, Amelia and Gwen let him do so. Soon after starting up the mountain, the road narrowed with virtually no shoulder along most of the cliff side. There was nothing ahead but a winding lane and nothing behind except more of the same.

Amelia's grip tightened on the steering wheel. Her oversized, unwieldy sedan had trouble holding the road. In the rearview mirror, she spotted a pickup truck with flashing lights. Assuming the driver wanted to pass, she thought about pulling over, but it was much too dangerous.

"It's so deserted here except for our tailgater," Gwen said, apprehensively.

"I know—I wish I could get out of his way. He's making me anxious." Amelia looked again into her rear view mirror. The truck was closer.

"Oh gees—this is not a place to get into an accident. My side has a steep drop with no visible bottom," Gwen announced.

"I'll move over just as soon as I can."

A safe stretch of shoulder was ahead. As Amelia drove nearer, she saw a huge wooden spool of wire unwinding and snaking in her direction. There was nowhere to drive but over the impending danger. Both axles tangled immediately, locking the wheels into a skid. Amelia feared they would slide off the precipice. She braced for the inevitable—but it didn't happen—the car got stuck in deep snow at the edge of the road.

The truck behind stopped and the driver climbed out. Dressed in a hooded sweatshirt, he waved a metal object. Gwen turned to get a look at the man's face and recognized him instantly. "That's the man I saw in the diner. He's holding a weapon!"

Amelia slid down in her seat as the hooded man approached her window. She grabbed the camera and snapped a few pictures of their potential murderer. The sound of ejecting photos jolted Amelia, rocking the car. She imagined it was set in motion toward their demise. Looking directly at the stranger, she expected the worst of the worst. But instead of a weapon, he was holding a wire cutter, and motioned she turn off the engine. He kneeled down on the snow-covered road and began cutting. One snip at a time, he pulled out pieces of deadly wire, enough to have spun Amelia's car into the gorge. She breathed a deep sigh of relief. "It's amazing. What are the chances of this happening?"

"Maybe he's an angel, showing up at the right time." Gwen wondered if he really could have been the same guy in the diner. "Angels appear out of nowhere," she quoted Daphne.

Amelia watched the stranger walk to his truck. He turned it around in the opposite direction, of all things, toward the base of the mountain. "What's he doing? Why is he going back? I must get a picture of his license plate before he's gone. Somehow, we have to thank him for saving our lives."

Without looking at the previous photos or the new one Amelia took of the truck, Gwen gathered them in a pile and slipped them over the visor.

"What just happened?" Amelia asked, settling into driving again.

"I think it has something to do with the package in the trunk."

Amelia shivered—maybe Gwen was right. Up ahead was a sign with an arrow pointing to Mount Hope Lodge. "We're here," Amelia laughed, thankful.

"Yeah, you, me—and the thing in the trunk," Gwen grumbled.

CHAPTER 23

Puzzle Pieces

A MELIA AND GWEN'S incident on the mountain road was dramatic enough for Daphne to assume it was related to her nightmares of impending danger. After a restful sleep, she awoke early. For a long time, Daphne just sat on the bed holding the package her students delivered. She untied the twine securing the brown paper and let it open, revealing a leather portfolio. Daphne ran her fingers back and forth over Arthur's name, feeling as though she was carrying a crucial piece of a puzzle. She played with the lock until something influenced her to rewrap the package and place it in her bureau drawer. Daphne dozed until daybreak.

She dreamed about driving a car with a passenger, a man she did not know. They came to a fork in their journey. To the right was a beautiful but treacherous mountain road that meandered through frozen surroundings. The left road led to an imposing arched bridge. The man wanted her to steer right because it was familiar. At the last minute, Daphne's car veered left.

The bridge ascended to the clouds. Daphne drove up and up, as if to Heaven, when at once, traveling full speed—she reached the crest. To her horror, the bridge was unfinished and hung in nothingness.

The vehicle careened into space. Daphne was certain they would crash to the rocks lining the gorge below. Just when it seemed hopeless, a sound of swooshing wings enveloped them—as though a gigantic dove arrived precisely at the right time.

Soaring in midair, the ride was joyous, peaceful, loving, and unlike anything either ever experienced. The man voiced his appreciation for taking the left turn. Once lowered to earth, a shooting arrow passed over him.

Daphne dressed to meet the others for breakfast. Amelia and Gwen wanted to identify the truck's owner by his license plate to express their gratitude. Daphne felt an indefinable gratitude of her own—the portfolio made it as well. Charles offered to drive the women to the constabulary office. The January morning air was crisp, and they zipped up to the chin until the valet brought the car to them.

"We'll need the photos from last night. They're still over the visor in Amelia's car," Gwen remembered.

"Can you get me the keys to the lady's sedan?" Charles asked the valet who responded promptly.

Charles drove them across the lot and let Gwen out. She reached inside Amelia's car for the pictures and grabbed the camera off the floor. "I have to turn this in at the lodge. Can we take care of it before going to the constabulary?" she asked Charles.

Charles had a sneaking suspicion the day was not going to be much to his liking. He patiently waited for Gwen to finish her business at the front desk, waving at rosy-cheeked skiers about to ride the lifts, wishing he was joining them. When Gwen was done, they drove to an official looking brick building with a sign: Mount Hope Constabulary. On the desk inside was a domed bell to tap, announcing their presence. An older man emerged and introduced himself as Deputy Byrne. He asked them to take a seat.

"Let's see the photographs before we make fools of ourselves," Amelia said, realizing they had not yet been examined. Gwen reached into her purse and handed them over. "Look—here it is—the license plate, as clear as the air outside today," Amelia acknowledged. She peeked at the other prints. The truck was there too, but no trace of the driver existed in any picture. Amelia decided to keep her baffling observation quiet for the time being.

Gwen began rubbing her eyes and stared at a cork bulletin board across the room. She got up to read Wanted posters and descriptions of missing persons. One flyer featured a young woman who disappeared from the lodge. Plucking it off the board, Gwen returned to her seat. "I can see this woman on a horse ranch out of state somewhere," she exclaimed.

When Gwen looked up, she met the astonished expression of Deputy Byrne who stood with his thumbs hooked into his gun belt, asserting his authority. The missing woman was a blemish on his otherwise spotless reputation. Foul play was one of the considerations, and investigators were banking on finding her body when the snow melted. Gwen's vision left the deputy flabbergasted. "What are you talking about—a horse ranch?" he interrogated her.

"I'm talking about this post," Gwen answered, showing him the flyer. "The woman is safe."

The deputy insisted Gwen come into his office. He closed the door. "Look, lady, I don't know what kind of a game you're playing here. What makes you think she's on a horse ranch?" he asked, eyeing her suspiciously.

"I can see her. It was planned—she knew the owner of the ranch and needed to escape her husband. If she hadn't, something terrible might have happened. Her husband was up to no good." Gwen spoke decisively, hoping it was not a problem for the woman to reveal her whereabouts.

The officer turned his back to her, dialed the phone, and muffled his voice as he spoke. "There's a lady in my office. I think she's some kind of psychic," was all Gwen could hear clearly.

Validation—Gwen was overjoyed a man with an official position was apparently willing to accept her abilities.

He hung up and swiveled around to face her, tapping his pencil on the desk. "I'm waiting for a call back. If you're right, I owe you big time. Wait in the front room with your friends," he said, opening the door for her.

The phone rang twenty minutes later. Deputy Byrne stepped out and addressed Gwen. "Ma'am, thank you. Now what can I do for you folks?"

Amelia came forward with a photo of the truck's license plate and briefly explained why they wanted the owner's name.

"Hmm…I don't know, it's not ethical," the deputy scratched his head. He reacted to Gwen's disappointment and changed his mind, inviting them into his office while he sent out a request for identification of the vehicle's owner.

As they waited for information to come over his Teletype, Deputy Byrne noticed how attractive Gwen was—petite, coppery hair, and a youthful complexion. He looked to see if she was wearing a wedding ring, but the flyer she was holding blocked his view.

"This makes no sense," he muttered to himself as he read the results of the inquiry. He sent out the request a second time, but received the same response. "Folks, the license plate number you gave me expired years ago. It belonged to a Dr. Arthur Wake."

"What?" Daphne and the others burst out simultaneously.

Charles pulled Daphne aside to discourage the conversation from progressing. He didn't want Franklin Port to further influence his vacation on Mount Hope. At first, Daphne resisted his suggestion, hoping there might be an explanation for the screwy events of recent times. Acquiescing, she thanked the officer and followed her friends out of his office.

Just before exiting the building, they noticed a hunched over, disheveled man who was not there before. He called to them in a drunken, slurred voice. "I know Arthur Wake. He owns the Mount Hope Lodge." He waved his finger, attempting to point the way.

Daphne and her group continued to the street, dismissing the man's words. They said nothing on the ride back to the lodge. Amelia kept the additional photos in her pocket until there was a better time to present them.

Gwen commented on the magnificent purple sky visible over the mountaintop. "I feel we've seen a beautiful sky like that before."

"I never have," Amelia told her.

A fleeting memory crossed Gwen's mind. A purple sky was shown to her last summer through the mirror in Daphne's turret. Gwen settled into the car's seat. She believed the sky was some kind of message that her psychic gifts might be needed right there on Mount Hope.

CHAPTER 24

The Portrait

T HE DRUNKEN MAN'S words kept ringing in Daphne's ears. She regretted ignoring him in the moment. When the foursome returned for lunch, she stopped at the front desk.

"Sir, is the owner of this lodge Arthur Wake?"

"No," the supervisor answered. "Artie Jeffreys owns the place—always has."

"Could I speak to him?"

"Forget it. Mr. Jeffreys never meets with guests—ever."

Daphne cocked her head, confused. She caught up with the group already seated in the dining hall. "The drunk was probably just shooting off his mouth. A man called Artie Jeffreys owns the lodge and is impossible to contact," she told the others, taking a seat next to Charles.

Before the meal was over, Gwen excused herself to inquire about the camera. "Did the person claim it?" she asked the young, freckle-faced clerk named Tommy.

He pulled it out and read the tag. "Sorry, no Jon Wassell is staying here. I searched the guest list three times, at least. I've asked around. There's nobody registered by that name."

"But the manager of the diner at the mountain's base said he was staying here."

"What diner is that?"

Overhearing the conversation, the supervisor interrupted. He assured Gwen the camera would find its way to the rightful owner. He took it from Tommy and waited until Gwen's back was turned before opening a closet filled with odds and ends. Most of the objects would be helpful if one was in dire straits traveling the mountain road—towing hooks, ropes, tire chains, flashlights, goggles, boots, and even a stack of warmer clothing for the less prepared. Now a camera was added to the mélange. Every tag had the same name—Jon Wassell.

"What are those things?" Tommy asked, bewildered.

"They're all from a diner at the foot of the mountain," his superior answered dryly.

"What diner?"

"Years ago, a diner burned to the ground when the lodge was first built," he replied, stone-faced. "The diner's manager died in the fire."

§ § §

When Gwen returned to the table, the remaining photos were spread across the surface. "What's happening here?" she wondered, looking at everyone's vacant expressions.

"It appears your hero last night was a ghost. Can you believe it?" Daphne bluntly asked.

"Believe it? Something unnatural is going on, for sure. It started with the package Jason gave us." Gwen began rubbing her eyes. She turned toward a large oil painting hanging over the fireplace. "I don't remember seeing that painting at breakfast." The others followed her gaze.

"I've had meals in this room since I arrived. It's new to me, too." Charles stood to get a better look at a beautiful portrait. Olivia 1896−1916 was on a brass nameplate affixed to the frame. "I wonder who Olivia is," he pondered out loud.

Daphne took notice of a jeweled clip holding the subject's upswept hair. It was exactly like the one she occasionally wore. "Olivia...Olivia... Olivia," she repeated, as though a bell was ringing in her head. Without explanation, she returned to the front desk. "I must see the owner of this lodge, Arthur Wake, or whatever you call him," she ordered the young clerk.

The supervisor dealt with the disturbance. "Madam, I already told you, there is no one here named Arthur Wake. But if you insist, leave a note, and I assure you I will personally deliver it to Mr. Jeffreys."

On the stationery provided, Daphne scribbled a simple note.

Dear Mr. Jeffreys,
I have something belonging to Dr. Arthur Wake. It is in my room—434.
Daphne Betel, Franklin Port

Daphne met up with her companions waiting at the elevator. The doors opened and they stepped in. "Where did you go?" Gwen asked.

"To the front desk—I wrote a note to the owner of the lodge."

"Why would you do that?" Charles criticized, tired of wasting time.

"The package Amelia and Gwen delivered contained a locked leather portfolio Jason found behind the walls of the Port Empress Inn. It was the property of Dr. Arthur Wake."

Charles was shocked—how could something found on his premises be given to Daphne? "Why the dickens didn't you tell us about it at breakfast?"

"The timing felt off."

Charles winced. "I don't get it."

In a way, Gwen thought she and Amelia were carrying a dead body in the trunk—something buried behind walls belonging to a man in his grave. "So, what was inside the portfolio?"

"I actually didn't open it," Daphne confessed.

"Let's get back to your suite and I'll open it," Charles commanded.

"But Charles, it doesn't belong to you."

"Last I heard, Arthur Wake was dead," he contested.

"I'm thinking he had a son who owns this lodge," Daphne stated. "And if that's true, the portfolio belongs to him." The elevator stopped on the fourth floor.

"The supervisor told you Artie Jeffreys owns the lodge. Why are you insisting otherwise?" Charles persisted.

"It was the name under the portrait, Olivia."

"What kind of a clue is that?" Amelia probed once they settled into Daphne's suite.

"The name triggered a memory of something written inside a notebook I found in my Victorian's attic, belonging to the former owner."

"And what does that have to do with the portfolio?" Charles asked, exasperated.

"The notebook had Olivia written inside. I'm realizing for the first time Olivia was Dr. Wake's wife. The formulas for my health and beauty lines are in that notebook belonging to her, not him."

Amelia and Gwen stared at each other. They never knew how Daphne created so many fine products leading to her wealth.

A rush of thoughts flooded Daphne's head. "They could have had a son named Arthur, nicknamed Artie. He and the owner of the lodge might be one and the same," she continued.

"Why would the owner call himself Artie Jeffreys if he's actually Arthur Wake Jr.?" Charles puzzled.

"I don't know why he wouldn't use his father's last name. Maybe Jeffreys was his mother's maiden name, who knows? All I need is an invitation to come face to face with Artie Jeffreys to be certain of the facts."

Daphne's unwavering conviction was winning out. Charles stroked the stubble on his chin, fighting his sense of ownership over the portfolio. "Daphne, if Dr. Wake had a son, why weren't you aware of him when the estate was settled and you bought the house?"

"The realtor said nothing about an heir."

"This is foolishness," Charles sighed.

"Just be patient until we see what happens," she encouraged. "I think Arthur Wake is the owner of this lodge—I mean Arthur Wake Jr."

"If it's true, I guess you do have to pass the package off to him," Amelia said, giving in.

"Yes, because it really wouldn't belong to any of us, would it?"

"What will convince you?" Charles persevered.

"Meeting him…"

They sat in tufted leather chairs and munched on a courtesy assortment of cheese and crackers. Charles made himself a stiff drink at the suite's small bar. To say the least, this trip was getting worse by the day.

"We're like mice in a maze, looking for cheese," Amelia thought out loud, sorting through the whole thing.

Charles threw his hands up, obviously not too pleased with the analogy.

"To get to the prize, we have to think cheese with every decision we make. But what is the prize, Daphne?" Amelia questioned.

"Consider it this way. If Artie Jeffreys is not the son of Dr. Wake, the prize belongs to us—we get to open the portfolio," she promised.

"I should get to open it," Charles corrected, almost choking on his cheese. "It was found on my property."

"Listen, this could be unfinished business for a departed soul, aka—Dr. Wake. So often, those who are still alive are being used to make things right for the ones who have crossed over. Let's go with the flow. As Amelia said, only think cheese. By evening, I'm certain we will have some kind of prize."

"I hope it's not more cheese," Charles mumbled, preferring to have the portfolio.

They played cards, snoozed, and chatted about changing politics for the better part of the afternoon. Once the waiting seemed pointless to everyone, a heavy knock sounded on the door.

CHAPTER 25

Alas!

MUCH TO EVERYONE'S relief, the night bellhop arrived at 6:45 PM, carrying a sealed note. They perked up. "Read it," Amelia insisted.

Daphne ripped it open and read aloud.

Daphne Betel
Be at the front desk—7PM
Artie Jeffreys

Without speaking another word, Daphne went to the bureau where she kept the package. Pulling it out, she momentarily held it to her heart. "Wish me luck. I'll be back," she said, leaving her suite.

"I see more wine and cheese in our future," Gwen joked.

"I used to like wine and cheese, but after this, it's coming off the menu at the Inn forever," Charles moaned, done with the whole Wake family business.

§ § §

Daphne handed the note to the supervisor. While he escorted her down a long corridor, she hoped things would be cleared up after speaking to Artie Jeffreys—no—Arthur Wake, she corrected herself. The supervisor opened a door for Daphne. His stern expression signaled she didn't belong inside the room. Ignoring him, she walked forward and stood still until he closed the door.

The dimly lit office was austere compared to the décor of the lodge. Daphne scanned its few contents. Most prominent was a Victorian walnut desk and a shadow of a man sitting behind it. A half-empty bottle of liquor and one glass was in front of him. The man's frosty countenance was disconcerting, as though drained of all life. He made no attempt to greet her. Daphne took a few steps in his direction nevertheless. She saw him glance at the package in her hands, and before he could look up again, she was already sitting on the opposite side of his desk, like a schoolgirl in the principal's office.

"Arthur Wake?" Daphne asked. "You are Arthur Wake Jr. from Franklin Port, aren't you?"

He didn't even blink at the name. For a fleeting moment, Daphne thought she made a serious error in reasoning, but despite that, she placed the package on the desk and pushed it toward the statue of a man. He still didn't move.

"This belongs to you," she said softly.

Something whispered in her ear. "Look to your left."

Her eyes rested upon a model ship protected under a glass dome. It was a schooner, much like the spectral vision appearing at her Fourth of July parties. The model had the name Olivia boldly painted on its starboard side. An inscription was illuminated with golden letters on the base:

December 24, 1921
Happy Fifth Birthday, AJW
Uncle Simon

Daphne's mind churned. She read about Arthur's brother, Simon, on the walls of The Port Empress Inn. Now she knew Dr. Wake did have a son and he was in the room with her. She sat back. Her body stiffened as she grabbed the arms of the chair. Her heart was in her throat because of some unexpected emotional connection to the tense, unhappy man.

The model ship was sitting atop a handsome, carved mahogany bookcase with a brass caduceus embellishing its highest shelf. The bookcase triggered another explosion of buried memories—it was the same one in her attic that had obscured the turret door. Daphne's mind dug deeper. Overwhelmed, she fought back anything more.

Daphne looked at the withered man behind the desk, strangely feeling love for him. However, it was obvious there would be no dialogue between them, so she stood to leave. She caught him appearing eager to untie the package, but he waited for her to exit.

Daphne entered her suite and explained to the others only what she knew for certain—Dr. Arthur Wake had a living son who is the lodge's owner. But what was inside the portfolio and why the son became known by another name remained a mystery. Charles was terribly disappointed she came back empty-handed and did not care much about her story.

For all the years Daphne traveled to Mount Hope with Sophia, she thought it was to find Jason's father among the guests. She could not have been more mistaken. Daphne dreaded making the crushing phone call to her childhood friend.

The day was a long, roller coaster ride, and Amelia was eager to return to the wetlands where life was more predictable. She and Gwen announced they were leaving for Franklin Port the next morning. Daphne was concerned their visit wasn't very enjoyable and promised to make it up to them.

§ § §

Gwen opened the door to her room, ready for a good night's sleep. She was greeted by a huge bouquet of fresh flowers placed on a round table, delivered while she was sequestered in Daphne's suite. A note from Deputy Byrne was pinned to the ribbon, thanking her for the accurate psychic tip. He also mentioned a position in his office, perfect for her, in the event she was thinking of making any life changes sometime soon. Gwen smiled, planning to contact him in a few weeks.

CHAPTER 26

Déjà Vu

D APHNE MADE CERTAIN Amelia and Gwen had a thermos of hot coffee to keep them alert on their trip. "Call me when you're safely home," she said, hugging them goodbye.

Amelia and Gwen were the only people traveling so early. The ride was easier on the way down the mountain, and the women looked forward to stopping for a hearty breakfast. They reached the base. "Where is the diner?" Amelia asked.

"Keep going, we're bound to run into it."

Already on the highway, they never passed the eatery. Gwen squinted and jerked forward, cupping her hands over her ears, shaking her head. She sat back with a peaceful expression, answering someone. "Yes, yes, I'm beginning to understand. He does need help."

Amelia pulled over and stopped the car. She checked the back seat to be sure they were alone. "Who are you talking to?"

"I think Daphne's ghost is giving me information," Gwen marveled.

"Oh come on, enough crapola."

"Seriously…be quiet…let me hear what he's saying."

Amelia put the car in park and sat there glaring at Gwen as though she lost her marbles.

"He's telling me there is no diner. There was one, but it burned down in a gas explosion, years ago."

"As I recall, we ate in a diner on our trip up. I don't get it. You're making me nuts with your psychic stuff."

"I'm not exactly sure how to explain this, but the diner appeared to us because we were going to need a camera. Do you remember the wire on the road and the photo you took of the truck?"

"Of course, of course—but you're not making any sense. How did we eat at a place you're saying isn't there?"

"Amelia, it can't make sense in this world when another world is overlapping. The diner is a portal for a father to show love to his son by making certain the son's business thrives against adversity. But remember, the father is from the Other Side."

Amelia laughed, almost maniacally. "Did the food have any calories? Because if it didn't, let's find the diner and eat. All kidding aside, was the camera real?"

"Who knows, but it helped put the portfolio into the rightful owner's hands."

"So…was the wire real?" Amelia persisted.

"I don't know—he's not talking anymore. I think you interrupted him with your laughing, Amelia."

The two women dissolved into giggles and got back on the highway with no further ado.

§ § §

Alone at last, Daphne and Charles made small talk. Daphne was relieved, having put to rest the dilemma of the portfolio. Charles was stifling his frustration. He believed the portfolio's contents might have helped answer why he felt so connected to Franklin Port's shoreline. On a whim, he sold his lucrative city restaurant to purchase Simon Wake's shabby, waterfront mansion. The renovations were extensive and ongoing. He hoped to discover more secrets behind the walls as soon as he returned home—anything to explain his fixation with Franklin Port.

Charles suggested they pass time by sitting in the dining hall, waiting for breakfast service to begin. The room was dark except for a faint glow in the fireplace. Shades covered floor-to-ceiling glass walls overlooking the slopes. The only sign of life was an employee or two working the graveyard shift. While Daphne and Charles sat there, she became ill at ease and asked him if they could take another seat—away from the portrait.

"What's wrong, Daphne?"

"Do you remember the late night conversations we used to have at my Victorian?"

"About converting my place to an Inn and getting the restaurant started?"

"No, I'm talking about when you were struggling with what you called your crazy thoughts and would ask me to help you make sense of them."

"Why are you bringing this up?"

Charles clearly remembered those discussions. At first, he sought out Daphne on the pretense he was interested in the architectural details of her sister Victorian. But in truth, his attraction to her and Franklin Port was far deeper. When he discovered she was a gifted psychic, a woman who helped people understand outlandish thoughts, he began to trust her with his unrelenting preoccupation.

At the time, he was haunted by an uncanny connection with the ship captain whose reported carelessness sank the Port Empress a century before. It was a conundrum Daphne could not resolve. Charles looked at the portrait and wondered how Olivia might be causing a similar discomfort for Daphne. What were her crazy thoughts?

"Daphne, every old house has previous owners—yours, mine, even Amelia's wetlands property. Now you know Dr. Wake had a wife and child. It's what anyone would expect. Why is it upsetting you?"

"I can't explain it any more than you could explain your ship captain obsession," Daphne sighed, knowing full well she wouldn't tell Charles about being in love with a ghost.

His words suddenly hit her—Arthur had another love and with her, a son. Never in a million years did Daphne think she could be jealous of a dead woman. Then it really hit her—Arthur and Olivia had each other on the Other Side. All he wanted was to get the damn portfolio to their living descendant. Arthur played her for a fool, thinking she'd never figure it out. The look on Daphne's face changed so abruptly, Charles didn't know what was happening.

"Let's move to another table right now," she pleaded.

Charles escorted her to a remote corner. His gentle touch along the small of her back felt soothing. Once seated again, a waiter approached and poured them coffee from a steeping hot brew. Daphne wrapped her hands around the mug, sipping slowly while looking back at the portrait that upset her so. It was no longer there.

She watched Charles drinking his coffee. She knew he was a good man. His thick, brown hair with streaks of silver was always neatly trimmed. She loved his smile when they hugged hello and goodbye. Charles took such care with everything. His kindness awakened something in Daphne she put to rest after her marriage failed, never thinking she could open her heart again.

"A penny for your thoughts," Charles asked, but she remained quiet.

Charles wished he could second-guess Daphne, just once. He longed to become her lover and protector, but always hit a wall. For Charles, trying to capture Daphne was like running after dandelion fluff in the wind—one is never able to hold the entire cluster once it becomes a hundred different pieces.

"I have something special for you I was saving for just the right moment," he said. Daphne watched him remove a small, velvet box from the side pocket of his herringbone, tweed sports coat. He placed it on the table.

"What is this?" she fluttered.

"Your chocolates are only temporary."

"What are you talking about?"

With that, Charles opened the box and an array of silver and gold coins, embossed with the shapes of her favorite dream symbols, tumbled out. They clinked and clanked as they hit the table and one another. Daphne fingered each one, awed by his thoughtfulness.

"How beautiful—these are intentions in silver and gold. Whatever made you think of this?"

"I wanted something more permanent for you because your chocolates are gone in an instant." Charles smiled. The lines around his eyes deepened in an endearing way. "I made another dream symbol for myself—one you have never used." Daphne watched him reach into the neck of his sweater and pull out a silver chain with a rectangular pendant for her to see. "This is my dream. It hasn't come true for me yet."

Embossed on the tag was Daphne's own greatest fantasy, a knight on a horse. She took his face in both her hands and kissed him on the lips for the first time ever.

Sunday, January 4

I should be grateful to Charles, especially since he revealed his dream to me. I would love him to be my knight in shining armor and give him my heart in return, but I have something to take up with Arthur first. ~D~

CHAPTER 27

Coming Home

CHARLES LET JASON know he and Daphne would be returning to Franklin Port in a few days, rather than the end of January. Jason freaked. The destruction caused by searching for the pivoting panel needed time to be repaired. He informed Charles the renovation was going badly and could not be completed on short notice, not with a snowstorm already underway. Jason was told to stop work immediately, no matter what state things were in. The timing was perfect for Charles. Anything else found in those walls belonged to him.

Jason returned to the Victorian to shovel the driveway before more snow accumulated. A commotion on the street distracted him. Several cars were honking at someone stuck on the road. With shovel in hand, Jason cleared the ice beneath the disabled car's rear wheels. Four bald tires kept spinning, going nowhere. Impulsively, he opened the driver side door and threw his shovel to the back seat. "Slide over, let me do it," he ordered.

He rocked the car back and forth until the wheels found traction and pulled forward. The windshield was frozen and visibility was nil. Jason fiddled with the dials to find the defroster, oblivious to the person sitting beside him.

"It doesn't work," she said, her words shaky from shivering. "The defroster, the heater—nothing works."

Jason braked at the stop sign. He looked at the young woman nestled in a hooded parka. "Cassie?" he asked, gently lifting the hood off her face.

Cassandra drew the hood forward again, humiliated to be caught in a state of desperation—especially by Jason. He jumped out to scrape ice off the windshield, and when he got back inside noticed the gas gauge on empty. They barely made it to the station.

"Fill 'er up," Jason told the attendant.

"No, no, put in only two dollars of gas," Cassandra called out the window while fumbling through her purse to find enough change.

"Let me take care of things," Jason said, opening her door and escorting

125

her to the station office where a kerosene heater was blazing hot. "Stand here—don't move."

Cassandra watched him return to the pumps and talk to the attendant, a friend of hers from the food pantry. She hoped he didn't reveal where she lived—that would be worse than anything. Cassandra saw her friend point in the direction of the mill. Her heart sank—Jason would be driving her home.

Jason paid with a twenty dollar bill and left the change on the dashboard. He brought Cassandra back to the freezing car, holding her against himself by opening one side of his jacket. Upon arriving at the mill, nearly deteriorated beyond recognition, Jason cringed to think Cassandra lived on its grounds. He parked her car in the bungalow's front yard. As her foot stepped into several inches of snow, she realized Jason needed a ride home. "It's almost dark. How are you getting back?"

"Do you have a couch in there?" he asked, motioning toward the bungalow. His eyes twinkled against a gray background of overcast weather and the decrepit mill looming behind.

"Yes..."

"Then it's settled, I'm staying here for the night."

His words went through her, terror, fear, dread—exhilaration, finally! Cassandra caught her breath—her dream was coming true.

The full moon had a white haze circling it. Jason put his arms around her. He lifted her chin to place a soft kiss on her lips. Bathed in the spell of icy moonlight filtering through clouds, neither of them wanted the moment to end. The air became still as it readied to unburden itself of yet another round of snow. There was a feeling of calm before the storm when one has no control of what is to be and is held captive by the working of Nature's grand scheme.

Moments later, they entered the bungalow, and her dog made a bee-line for Jason, dropping a toy at his feet. "Amigo is shy. I'm surprised he's being so friendly," Cassandra remarked.

"I always dreamed of having a pet someday." While stroking the tail-wagging creature, Jason looked around the living room, impressed by how cozy and stylish it was. His place was a crash pad, nothing more. In contrast, here was a young woman who made a welcoming nest with very little means.

Lost in thought, something tugged at his conscience. Cassandra deserved more than what he originally had on his mind. She was different,

126

and everything about the situation was different. He couldn't identify this strange new emotion, having played the field with the ladies for a long time.

"Amigo needs to go out," Cassandra said, hooking a leash to her dog's collar.

Jason raised a finger for her to wait a minute. He walked over to a small table with a record player and a stack of 45s next to it. "May I?"

She nodded, and he sifted through the records before choosing the perfect song to play, snapping the plastic disk in place for the turntable's spindle. Cassandra enjoyed seeing him at ease. He turned the volume high, grabbed her free hand, and pulled her and Amigo outside into the chilly night. She let go of the leash. In the sweet fire of youth, Jason held her tightly. She rested her head on his chest. Dancing to the music, he led her into a faster tempo and turned her under his uplifted arm. Cassandra spun again and again until he let go. Dizzy, she fell into his open arms—a spark was ignited. The record ended, breaking the spell.

Jason stayed outside with Amigo gathering enough logs from the woodpile to last them through night. While he was out, Cassandra changed the record to one of her favorites. She smiled at how many times she played that love song and thought of Jason. Now, after all was said and done, he was right there. It confirmed to her there must be magic in the Universe to make dreams come true. Cassandra was happy she didn't let pride get in its way and was glad Jason drove her home. A powerful feeling rippled through every fiber of her being. Her destiny was to be with Jason.

Cassandra heated a pot of homemade stew. Both she and Jason took on tasks until it was time to sit at the wooden table and eat. It was covered with one of her mother's linens, set with two bowls, forks, and cups. Everything was falling into place as if it had always been. Jason felt he found a safe harbor—home. Her little bungalow showed loving touches reflecting a quality he suspected was in her. For that reason, Jason made sure to appear at the Victorian on afternoons he thought she might be there for class. The electricity in the air whenever their eyes met was enough to set his world on fire, but the night of Daphne's banquet stirred something much deeper in his soul.

Music filled the room and minutes passed without either of them speaking a word. Jason stared at Cassandra—she was beautiful, with cheeks flushed from the cold. Her bright smile melted him. He lifted his fork and leaned closer to feed her. She closed her eyes. It felt natural to accept his loving gesture, trusting Jason unlike anyone she ever trusted before.

"Cassie," he spoke.

Her eyes remained closed, her heart skipping a beat. The moment was magical.

He paused, knowing this woman would give him the family he always wanted. He could be the father he never had. In the enchantment, time stood still. Jason asked, "Cassie, will you marry me?"

CHAPTER 28

Fire!

DAPHNE'S HOLIDAY ON Mount Hope changed her world. So many years were spent tracking down Jason's father, when, instead, she was being led to Arthur's own son. She had to know why he was so deceptive, keeping his agenda a secret. Her first week back home, she walked the corridors of the Victorian night after night, expecting Dr. Arthur Wake to provide answers.

When he did not respond to her growing dismay, she fumed, shouting for him to show up in the library, pick out a book, or give her inspiration. Even chocolate making didn't work. No calming purple plume or sweet whisperings took place. It seemed he was done with her now that the portfolio was given to his precious, detached son. Feeling bereft and exhausted, Daphne let very little into her world. She refused to resume classes.

The news of Cassandra and Jason's engagement reached her. Throwing a party in their honor would be exactly what she needed to lift her spirits, and she mailed invitations for the last evening in January.

§ § §

When Charles returned to the mess at his Inn, it sent him into a sleepless frenzy for days. Unable to lay his fury to rest over the portfolio, he searched the floorboards and walls for more hidden objects.

Daphne interrupted Charles from going berserk by unexpectedly appearing on his doorstep. She noticed her party invitation on a stack of unopened letters. "You didn't open this," she scolded, picking up the envelope and waving it.

"Daphne," his hollow voice pleaded. It was the same voice she heard when he struggled with his crazy thoughts. "Help me. I'm drowning."

"What's happened here?" she puzzled, taken aback by the shambles. In a matter of speaking, Charles was drowning, but in a sea of debris he created. She acted quickly, knowing another world was colliding with his reality, and ripped open the invitation. "Here, read this."

He read it aloud three times before reacting. "Jason is marrying the farm girl?" he asked.

"Yes, he proposed while we were away. I want to take Cassandra, Gwen, and Amelia to the finale of the Franklin Port Theater's winter production. Jacquelyn has the lead part and left me tickets. You do remember Jacquelyn, don't you?"

Charles blinked hard. Her name put him on track.

"I'll entice Cassandra back to my house afterwards for a small surprise party. But I need your help."

"I'm afraid I can't be of help to anyone right now," Charles pined.

"Quite the contrary, I want you and Jason to oversee the setup, that is, if your kitchen is still intact and your staff would like to make money." She thought it dubious, considering the condition of the Inn, but to her surprise, Charles nodded in agreement, too tired for any more details. He guaranteed to make it happen.

§ § §

On the night of the finale, all three women arrived at the Victorian, bundled up for a short walk to the theater with Daphne. The house was dark when they left. Minutes later, the Inn's caterers brought assorted chafing dishes and a heart-shaped cake with Cassandra and Jason's names written in butter cream icing. Chandeliers lit darkened rooms and smoke billowed from chimneys. Guests arrived with decorations in the theme of the coming Valentine's Day. They strung glittery, cutout hearts over doorways and scattered shiny, wrapped candies on tables along with sparkling confetti everywhere. Red, helium-filled balloons held with long ribbons danced on the backs of Daphne's chairs. On cue, everyone hid, waiting for Cassandra's entrance.

§ § §

Jacquelyn's debut as actress and singer was a huge success. The audience loved her—a new talent, a sensation from out of nowhere, the critics heralded. Daphne's group rose to their feet in applause as the final curtain dropped to close the season. They looked at each other, never imagining Jacquelyn could be so well received. She greeted them at their seats, still dressed in full costume and makeup. When Daphne invited Jacquelyn for coffee and cake at the Victorian, Cassandra withdrew a bit, but Daphne squeezed her hand and whispered all was well.

"I'll meet you there later," Jacquelyn said. "I have to get out of this costume first."

The women walked back to Daphne's house. When it came into view, Amelia saw it wasn't dark anymore. "What's going on in your house?" she asked, pretending to not know about Cassandra's surprise party.

"Oh, I asked Charles to drop by with dessert for us, that's all." Daphne brushed off the question.

Cassandra seemed concerned. "Look, Daphne, there's even a light in your turret. Who could be up there?"

Daphne stopped walking, surprised Cassandra observed something supernatural. Only Daphne knew there was no electricity in the turret. "It's just a reflection of the moon," she explained, hoping Cassandra did not pursue the issue. Daphne was furious—Arthur's timing was awful. She had a bone to pick with him, if only he would stay put until the end of the party.

The women entered the warm house. Jason stood there, all spruced up, wearing khaki pants and a blue, button-down collar shirt under an argyle vest. It was a first for Cassandra to see him so polished. "What's going on?" she asked suspiciously.

Her friends jumped from behind couches, chairs, and drapery. "Congratulations!"

"Is this for me?" Cassandra placed both hands along the sides of her face in astonishment.

"Yes!" they cheered.

Daphne put a record on her stereo and the party began. Once the food was down to its last delicious morsel, everybody sat around to watch Cassandra open exquisitely wrapped engagement gifts. She never owned such beautiful things—china place settings, crystal stemware, fine linens, and such.

As Cassandra was about to slice the cake, Jacquelyn walked in. She strutted closer to the table. Her full-length coat slipped off her shoulders, revealing a close fitting, white knitted sweater and calf-length black skirt. High-heeled black boots completed the look. Her long blonde hair flowed down her back, and she was still wearing much of the makeup and jewelry from the stage. Jacquelyn, indeed, looked like a movie star.

The cake knife Cassandra held, covered in sticky icing, slipped from her hand and fell onto the Oriental rug. Embarrassed, she stooped to wipe it and missed seeing Jason's reaction to the newly discovered celebrity.

Jason felt he was hit by a stun gun. Everything could be ruined if Cassandra ever found out about Jacquelyn and him at the Inn. He helped Cassandra to her feet, acting as if he hadn't seen the budding star. But in truth, he was rattled beyond words. Jacquelyn deliberately moved closer to Jason to get her dessert first, once it dawned on her what the celebration was about. Their eyes met. Cassandra noticed.

Feeling threatened, Cassandra threw down the knife and walked into the parlor to be with other guests, but thought twice about leaving her fiancée and that flirt together. She went back to stake her claim on Jason. Unfortunately, she overheard Jacquelyn question him with a belittling tone.

"You're marrying her?"

Jason saw Cassandra in the doorway and ignored Jacquelyn's question. He reached out to his bride-to-be, not knowing what else to do. For the first time, he wondered if glamour would better serve his needs than substance. Cassandra unexpectedly extended her hand to Jacquelyn, congratulating her for a stellar performance, but Jacquelyn snubbed the gesture. Cassandra's good manners did not go unnoticed by Jason.

The party was shortened due to a sudden storm. Jacquelyn was the first to leave the Victorian, realizing she hit a dead end with Jason—one more time.

§ § §

Charles remained with Daphne until the last person left. About to kiss her good night, he heard fire engines coming into her yard. The moment was lost. Several firemen in heavy suits and carrying axes barged through the Victorian's back door. "Get everyone out! Your house is on fire! Get out! Get out!" the chief shouted.

The baffled couple stumbled into the backyard. Looking up to the turret, they saw flames shooting out from its pointed roof as snow fell around them. Brilliant amber light filled the windows—Daphne's house was ablaze.

CHAPTER 29

A Sepia Past

WHEN THE LAST fireman left the premises, Daphne and Charles hobbled through the back door on numb feet, only to find the kitchen filthy with slushy footprints and outlines of hoses dragged through the house.

"Oh, Daphne, this is dreadful—totally dreadful!" Charles lamented, examining the mayhem. "Did the fireman you spoke to find a cause for the fire?"

"There was no fire." Her voice was low.

"I don't understand. We saw flames with our own eyes."

"I know, but they were only to catch our attention—not real fire."

"How can that be?"

"We might have answers if you come to the turret with me."

Dog tired, Charles was beyond arguing and plopped into a chair. "Give me a minute."

Daphne pulled him to his feet. She was beside herself thinking Arthur was ready to explain why he deceived and abandoned her, but could not face the ghost alone. "It will all make sense," she said, pushing Charles to the staircase.

When they reached the attic, an amber glow appeared under the turret door. Charles stopped, not knowing what to make of it—was he being driven crazy by Daphne's house too? He stumbled as she shoved him forward. The door opened and they were sucked in. The door closed. In the middle of the shadowy space, the old mirror emitted a somber sepia light, revealing cinematic images and stories of the past.

1915—"I now pronounce you man and wife. You may kiss your bride."

The groom turned to his heart's devotion and tenderly placed his lips on hers, communicating the fullness of his love for all eternity.

"Arthur, you are my knight in shining armor," Olivia professed lovingly, adoring him for being so protective. Her face was luminous.

"And you, my dear one, complete me," he responded.

133

A setting, mid-August sun shone down onto the exquisite Austrian crystals painstakingly hand sewn to the bodice of the bride's ivory-colored silk gown.

Arthur basked in Olivia's radiance, but struggled with a forlorn thought. "If you ever leave me, I could not bear the loss and would become but a shell of a man."

"We will be together forever," she assured her husband.

"You must promise to always be mine," he begged.

"Yes, I will be yours for eternity."

Underneath a beautiful arbor in the old homestead, they greeted many friends and the bride's family, the Jeffreys. No one from the Wake family attended the wedding, as the only living relative, Simon, refused the invitation. His conspicuous absence tormented the groom.

"Simon's rejection is disturbing you, not to mention all the other things he has said and done to hurt you. I can feel it," Olivia spoke softly.

Arthur Wake forced a smile to offset her concerns. "Nonsense, my love, all that Simon stole from my parents' estate pales in comparison to the treasure I have in you." He pulled her hand to his heart and gently kissed it. "We have our lovely Victorian, my growing medical practice, and hopefully, a family of our own very soon."

Arthur's eyes twinkled at the thought of his wife bearing him a child. Olivia felt inseparable from him, but was deeply troubled by the serious rift between her husband and his younger brother—over her.

§ § §

When Simon returned from his service at sea to pay a final farewell to his dying father, he was told of Olivia's engagement to Arthur. Because Simon also had feelings for her, he was enraged with himself for keeping them secret. On that very trip home, he intended to ask Olivia for her hand in marriage, but it was too late—she already accepted his brother's proposal.

So jealous and incensed by the news of their engagement, Simon convinced his father that Arthur was unworthy of handling the estate. Simon requested to be named executor of the family's fortune with privileges to act as he saw fit.

Revenge against Arthur was all Simon thought about, even if it took the rest of his life. He invented a story claiming Olivia was his fiancée and Arthur stole her. Simon recited this mistruth in the local pubs, attempting to destroy his brother's reputation. Arthur got calls in the middle of the night to drag an intoxicated Simon home. The brothers would have words, violent ones, which left rumors flying for years. There was nothing to be done—fate had intervened and Arthur and Olivia were to be married.

Simon cheated Arthur out of every dime of the family's wealth. The final blow was when he blatantly spent vast amounts of money building a waterfront mansion over the ruins of a coastal refuge station. It became the grandest residence in town, making him feel superior to his brother.

§ § §

After the wedding celebration, Arthur and Olivia went home to their Victorian to open the gift each had for the other. Arthur delighted in handing his bride a silver box. Her heart leaped. Inside was the diamond studded hair clip she saw at the jewelers where they bought their simple gold bands. She was surprised he even noticed her admiring it. "Oh Arthur, this was much too expensive."

"I'd do anything for you."

Arthur helped place it in her hair, his hand tenderly over hers. She threw her arms around his neck and kissed him with all her love before taking him into the round room on the first floor to reveal her gift to him. "I thought this should be your library," she said, opening the door for them to enter.

Olivia removed a sheet draped over a handsome mahogany bookcase with a prominent brass caduceus to represent his medical oath. She arranged for its delivery during the ceremony. Arthur knew she must have spent her last dollar on this beautiful piece of furniture. He would make it up to her, tenfold.

§ § §

1916—"Arthur, it looks like tomorrow might be a white Christmas." Olivia rubbed her swollen belly. "Have you finished your letter to Simon, inviting him to our holiday dinner?"

"Yes, my love, I finished it. But how many times before has Simon rejected us? What makes you think it will be any different?"

"It will be different because it has to be. Our baby will be born in less than a month, and I want him or her to know Uncle Simon."

The conversation was interrupted by a phone call. Arthur left the room to answer it. When he returned, he was wearing his overcoat and carrying his doctor's bag. "I have to visit a patient at her home. She thinks she's gone into labor. Wait for me, and we'll walk to Simon's house together, just as soon as I return."

Arthur kissed Olivia's forehead and stepped into the cold December air. It was the morning of Christmas Eve, and for a moment Olivia felt terribly alone. She sat at her husband's desk and read his handwritten note to Simon, adding a few words of her own at the bottom. The baby was more active than usual, and she found herself calming the unborn child with long, soothing strokes across her abdomen.

Olivia hadn't heard from Arthur all day and didn't know which patient he went to see. She began to fret—snow was accumulating on the ground and whipping winds blew through the Victorian's windows. On a whim, she walked to Simon's mansion to deliver the invitation.

While rapping on Simon's door, Olivia felt a sharp pain in her belly. She doubled over with the next one, far more intense than the first, as she frantically continued knocking. Searing pain ripped through her, and she began to bleed profusely. One hand held her abdomen against the contractions while she banged on the door with the other—leaving bloody prints. All became quiet.

Simon thought he heard someone at the door and rushed down two flights of stairs to open it. Horrified, he found Olivia lying motionless on the porch and caringly carried her inside. Her muscles tightened as labor progressed. Simon tried calling Arthur, but the phones went dead due to the storm.

Simon and Olivia were alone together for the first time, but he feared she was dying. He always longed to hold her—only not like this. On the coldest and darkest of winter nights, Olivia's boy child was born as she breathed her last, dying from loss of blood.

Simon was able to cut the umbilical cord and gingerly wrap the wailing infant in the warm flannel shirt he was wearing, as if the child was his own. He took the letter from Olivia's clenched hand, read it, and wept. Words in her handwriting ripped through his heart: Simon, I beg you, please make peace with your circumstances. Love poured through him, then remorse for all the anguish he caused the couple. It didn't have to be this way.

§ § §

1923 — "Father! Father! Uncle Simon is coming on his schooner. Can I go to the dock now?" Young Arthur Jeffreys Wake, nicknamed AJ, called up the Victorian's winding staircase.

The child was eager to spend July Fourth on his uncle's boat. He rarely had pleasurable times in his home life, attending boarding schools while his father buried himself in work. Arthur let AJ visit Simon twice a year — for the July celebration and the boy's birthday which fell on Christmas Eve. Arthur knew it was his late wife's wishes for Uncle Simon to be in AJ's life. Otherwise, he grew to despise Simon, blaming him for the loss of his beloved.

To avoid any contact with his brother, Arthur allowed his son to wait on the dock while he watched him from the turret. Just as the schooner lowered its sails and went under power, young AJ, in all his excitement, slipped off the dock and struggled for air as he bobbed in the churning water below. Arthur, in his white medical coat, raced down the stairs and through the back door. He ran with superhuman speed across the yard, leaving a wind on either side of him.

Arthur pulled his son from the water before the boat nearly killed them both. He scooped AJ into his arms and carried him to the Victorian, clinging to his dripping wet body. Once inside, young AJ could hear his uncle trying to gain entry, to resume the sailing plans they impatiently anticipated all year. Simon furiously pounded on the door with both fists and shouted, "This has to stop — he's all that's left!"

The wind chime rang turbulently. Behind the Victorian's door was an angry response, "Go away!" Arthur's refusal sent Simon away — forever.

By evening, Simon sat at his desk. He wrote and addressed a letter to Arthur, secured with sealing wax. He felt a moment of brotherly love and wanted to make amends, but a framed photograph of Arthur, Olivia, and himself during happier times caught his eye and rekindled his anger. He yanked the picture from its frame and scrawled a message across the back.

Simon became so disheartened, he thought otherwise about sending the letter. Instead, he stuffed it with the picture into a secret compartment in a wall where he stored a locked, leather portfolio. The letter was never mailed. Simon Wake fell into a deep sleep that night, not to awaken, as his broken heart ceased to beat.

137

§ § §

1937—AJ came of age, able to collect his inheritance from Uncle Simon's estate. The years away from home had taken a bitter toll on his relationship with his father. AJ never understood his father's torment, or knew the depths of love his father had for him through the coldness he was being shown. As time marched forward, his father never understood his son's hatred for him. AJ intended to cut all ties to Franklin Port as soon as his uncle's legalities were settled. He spent his evenings in a local bar and one night, barely made his way home.

Arthur tried to rouse his son from a drunken stupor, but AJ took a swing and landed on the floor. Infuriated, Arthur pulled him to his feet to force him outside for some cold air. "Get out," he yelled. "Come back when you're sober," Arthur demanded.

"I hate you and I'm never coming back," AJ shouted, as he grabbed his coat and papers and stormed out the door, never to be in contact with his father again.

§ § §

The images in the mirror blurred and disappeared, leaving Daphne and Charles in shock. "Now I understand why I had to see this for myself. The portfolio was not mine to have," Charles said, hoping to make peace with the experience.

Upon hearing his words, Daphne regretted her single-minded fervor to get the package to AJ, being insensitive to Charles. She realized how many other people she disregarded and placed second to Arthur—Marc, her daughters, and friends. She began to weep, uncertain of her role in anyone's life.

Concerned about Daphne's emotional entanglement with a ghost, Charles made an instant decision for himself. "I'm going to finish restoring the Inn and then rethink my future."

Daphne stepped back to look at him, suddenly fearing Charles, like the others, might not always be there. He was important to her, and she hoped it wasn't already too late. She regretted allowing Arthur to edge every-one out, and now worried how she could bear Charles abandoning her.

Returning to the parlor, they reentered reality. Recognizing how intrusive and restless spirits can be, Charles came to grips with his Inn being haunted. He resolved not to allow ghostly influences any longer. He left Daphne's house, finally feeling grounded.

As Charles got closer to the Inn, he experienced discomfort in his chest, as though something was putting pressure on it. Shallow breaths came quicker. Each exhalation froze at the tip of his nose. Being weary, all he could think about was getting home and crashing into bed, but the night had other plans for him.

Charles turned the key to the Inn's front door and stomped off clumps of snow before entering the lobby. He shook his head in dismay at the expensive repairs ahead. Without warning, he was propelled to one wall and then the opposite, as if on a rocking ship battered by powerful waves. He became nauseated. The sensation of water rising and heaving against his body overtook him. "We're sinking!"

The room filled with the sound of men bellowing raucous remarks and hoarse shouts. A stench of stale beer and vomit pervaded the air. Charles staggered to a doorway, clinging to exposed studs along the way. The once crisp, white cloths and crystal vases on the dining tables were covered with dust and debris. Floorboards were randomly pried up, and fine silk drapes were ripped off their rods, lying crumpled on the floor. "What do you want from me?" Charles screamed in despair, having no recollection of doing all this damage.

Two crystal vases spontaneously shattered, sending shards through the air. The entire room became active and the sounds unbearable. Objects propelled off shelves with trajectories aimed directly at him. Something came over Charles. He would no longer allow his life to be driven by ghosts. He shouted with conviction and determination coming from every sinew of his body. "GET OUT—NOW—DAMMIT! THIS IS MY PROPERTY AND I AM NOT LEAVING! YOU ARE LEAVING! OUT...OUT!"

The atmosphere lightened, the rocking ceased, and things stopped flying at him. Charles had taken charge and would no longer be at the mercy of spirits—or so he thought.

CHAPTER 30

Choose Again

WITHOUT DAPHNE'S SCHOOL in session, Gwen busied herself by returning to Mount Hope alone, in response to a formal letter from Deputy Byrne. He reminded her of his job offer and promised a substantial salary. It was too attractive for Gwen to ignore.

Driving steadily, she reached the foot of the mountain and laughed as the diner appeared. The manager stepped out, waving her over. She guessed she'd need something to make it to the top. He handed her a cellophane-wrapped package of chocolates with a raised image of a mirror on each one. She recalled the mirror in the turret. When she looked up, the man was gone. A shiver shot down her back. Driving away, Gwen glimpsed over her shoulder—no diner either. "No one would ever believe this," she said out loud.

The steep road was unrecognizable, the surroundings drastically changed. Gwen pondered whether this was due to winter storms or the ghost's influence. She came upon a dilapidated, wood-covered bridge spanning a deep gorge. The rickety crossing looked dangerous. Gwen drove forward with caution, baffled as to why she couldn't remember it from her last trip. Aged timbers groaned as the bridge sagged. Her wedding invitation fiasco crossed her mind. Gwen dismissed it as old challenges in the face of new ones. She breathed a sigh of relief once safely across.

Upon reaching the lodge, a bellhop escorted Gwen to a luxurious penthouse suite. The first thing she saw was a desk with another cellophane-wrapped package of chocolates. She paused to look around the room. "What's going on here?" Gwen asked the bellhop.

"Aren't your accommodations suitable?"

"Yes…but I can't afford to stay in this. I reserved a simple room."

The bellhop called the front desk to check. "No, madam, we have you registered for this suite—paid in full for as long as you like."

With that, the young man left. Gwen placed her chocolates from the diner next to those already there. The new package had an image of a bridge.

Surprisingly, things were beginning to make sense. "Doctor Arthur Wake, are you here? Are these chocolates and this suite of your doing?" Gwen asked, settling in. "Great, now I'm a kept woman—and by a ghost!"

Gwen tried phoning Daphne to let her know she returned to the mountain and to share other bits of mystery enveloping it, including symbols on chocolate. Not on the first, second, or even third try was Gwen able to reach her.

§ § §

Isolation can play tricks with the mind when harsh winds howl through cracks and crevices of an old building and long shadows fill dark spaces. Daphne ignored all calls, waiting nightly in the library for Arthur to show her some appreciation for delivering the portfolio to his son. Little did she know—Arthur's attention was on Gwen.

§ § §

The following morning, Gwen rushed through the lodge's lobby to make her appointment with the deputy. She bumped into a man, almost knocking him over. Gwen felt she had been pushed, although no one else was around them. "Excuse me," she apologized.

He reached down to pick up an official letter she dropped in the mishap and saw an address, Franklin Port, with a return address from Deputy Byrne. The man glared at Gwen and scowled. He seemed unable to catch his breath. She escorted him to the nearest chair and called for assistance.

"Are you all right, Mr. Jeffreys?" the supervisor asked, responding immediately to Gwen's urgent plea.

"Leave me alone," he barked at his employee.

When Gwen heard the name Mr. Jeffreys, she knew she was looking at Dr. Wake's son. She felt compelled to introduce herself, but he hurried away. Running late, Gwen proceeded to the Constabulary Office. A CLOSED sign in the window prompted her to walk the shoveled path around the building. She heard shouting through an open side door, as if someone just entered. Unable to avoid eavesdropping, Gwen recognized Mr. Jeffreys' voice.

"Who is she?" he hollered, enraged.

"She's a psychic, Art. We need her. I thought she could help figure out the lunacy on this mountain. Guests come into my office daily with one cockamamie story after another. Before you know it, this will become Mount Hopeless with the reputation it has."

"That name suits me fine, send her away. I know what's going on. I don't care if people stop coming. I don't care about you, this business, or anything else!"

Mr. Jeffreys' tone was distant, unyielding—as if stuck in a quagmire of hatred. Although his attitude was nothing new to the deputy, his hostility escalated since the New Year. The deputy's good intention caused his boss to be on the warpath.

Mr. Jeffreys stormed out, not seeing Gwen standing there. She watched the door being pulled shut. Her heart sank. Since Doctor Wake's son actually knew everything his father had been doing for him, she assumed something must have gone terribly wrong in his past or he would be grateful.

Gwen knocked on the side door, but the deputy didn't answer. Two more days passed and the CLOSED sign remained. She left a note in the deputy's mailbox explaining the mountain was haunted, and if he cared to know more, he would have to contact her in Franklin Port. Gwen packed her things and went to check out, hoping someone paid the bill, as the bellhop assured.

"Sorry, madam, there's no record of you being here," the desk clerk said after checking the registry several times.

"That's impossible. I stayed in the penthouse suite."

"No one has been in the penthouse since last season," Tommy politely argued. Gwen decided to walk away before the situation changed, when the clerk called after her. "Hey, aren't you the lady who left us the camera a month ago?"

Gwen ignored him. No sooner had she started her car, when it stalled and wouldn't restart. Sensing she was being deliberately detained, Gwen remembered being in the turret when the ghost told her, "Find him. Help him." She deduced the child in the mirror, who fell off the dock, must have been the ghost's son. Here she was on a mountain where she found him, but how could she possibly help him? Gwen considered writing another note, this one to Mr. Jeffreys, hoping her car would start if she did.

She went back inside and asked the desk clerk for stationery. Finding a comfortable spot away from everything, she stared at the walls trying to figure out the best way to write what needed conveying. She wanted Mr. Jeffreys to appreciate his father's love for him. The pile of discarded papers by her feet grew higher until Gwen remembered one of Daphne's most profound teachings—a tiny leaf of forgiveness will crumble a solid wall of resistance, as its impact is so great.

Since Mr. Jeffreys was aware his father's spirit was on the mountain, the problem must reside within Artie Jeffreys. Gwen was overcome with an inexplicable emotion—she and Mr. Jeffreys shared an uncanny bond, perhaps stemming from a deep loss at the beginning of their lives. But unlike her, it seemed he painted himself into a corner from which he couldn't escape.

She started writing again, and the words poured forth. They were simple—things happen to all of us, things we cannot control or understand. But what we can control is how we choose to respond—and that makes all the difference. She ended her note with the message she remembered illuminating across the Victorian's wall after the dance circle. Make peace with your circumstances.

Gwen knew those words provided a foundation for change, and if Mr. Jeffreys could replace bitterness with forgiveness, she helped him. Satisfied, she sealed the envelope, gave it to the clerk for Mr. Jeffreys, and left. Her car started right up. "Now, Dr. Wake, you have a gift for me, and I hope it's not more chocolate."

Her wedding invitations flashed across her mind again, forcing Gwen to make peace with her own circumstances.

CHAPTER 31

The Attic Trunk

GWEN RETURNED TO Franklin Port, concluding the only purpose of her trip was to meet Mr. Jeffreys. She hoped her note effectively provided the help Dr. Wake asked for, but even if it didn't, the experience inspired in her a fascination with town history. As if guided to uncover more, she spent many evenings pouring over archives and old newspapers at the library. Gwen wrote expanded versions of events found in village records, adding subtle bits of information from her psychic visions. She typed each vignette and made booklets, thinking something good would come of it.

A neighbor dropped by and noticed the growing collection on Gwen's desk. "What's all this?" Lillian asked, randomly picking up a finished story titled, Scandal on the Harbor.

Gwen was not sure how to explain herself to the head of the Franklin Port Historical Society, a woman known to be a stickler for factual details. "I have psychic abilities. I see human drama hidden between the lines," Gwen admitted, surprised by her assertive response.

Lillian pulled up a chair, wanting to hear more. She had the foresight to know revisiting bygone days would intrigue residents, and the Society could create cultural programs around Gwen's booklets, selling them as well. For Lillian, it was about generating money, rather than actually believing in ESP. She offered Gwen an opportunity to work with the Historical Society.

§ § §

Gwen briefly stopped by the Victorian, excited about sharing the news of her job. She found Daphne stirring the makings for chocolate in a double boiler on the stove. "It smells heavenly," Gwen said, moving closer for a better whiff. "Are you planning to hold classes again?"

"Not anymore," Daphne answered, less engaging with Gwen than usual.

Gwen spotted an old, well-worn notebook on the counter. "That book looks ancient," she commented.

"Yes, it was left behind by the estate." Daphne finished stirring the pot. She took in a deep breath and looked up as though something suddenly came to mind. Daphne thought about the day she found the chocolate molds and notebook in her attic. A faint memory of something else at the trunk's bottom struck her. She had an urge to rummage through the trunk again— but at another time.

Although Gwen was still eager to share her news, it could wait—she was now rushing to a meeting with the Historical Society.

§ § §

Daphne went to her cherished marble-top cupboard. On the shelves behind glass doors were ceramic labeled jars and bottles with tinctures, elixirs, liqueurs, and spices. She removed a copper mold with an image she never used before—the spiral. It felt just right. She poured the silky blend into the tray and placed it in the refrigerator to harden. "It's done."

§ § §

Sophia made arrangements to come to Franklin Port and take her future daughter-in-law wedding gown shopping. Pleased to be included in their venture, Daphne insisted Sophia stay in the Victorian with her. She passed the days cleaning the guest room—dusting and clearing cobwebs, happy for another reunion so soon after their disappointing trip to Mount Hope. Her friend arrived on the evening before their shopping excursion. Like young brides themselves, they prepared a list of salons between Franklin Port and the city.

Cassandra showed up at the Victorian in time for breakfast with the ladies. She looked over the list. Eager to shop, they headed out, but by the end of a long day, finding a bridal gown seemed fruitless. As Cassandra's spirits wilted, Daphne remained optimistic and drove them back to the local store for one more round of browsing.

"What brings you here again?" the bridal attendant asked.

"I know you're closing soon. We won't take long—just another look, if you don't mind," Daphne explained. A reluctant Cassandra dragged herself to the racks of gowns.

"No, dear, those are not your size or in your budget, as I remember," the woman said, squelching what was left of Cassandra's enthusiasm. "I told you so when you were here this morning."

Cassandra's heart dropped, and she was led to the rack suitable for her. Surprised, she saw a dress Jason would like—modest in its design. The attendant escorted her to the fitting room and helped her into the gown. Cassandra admired herself in the mirror. "This is perfect. Can I show the others?" she asked the woman.

"Wait one moment. Another bride is using the pedestal."

Cassandra remained in the fitting room, anticipating her turn to show the dress to Daphne and Sophia. The attendant came to get her. As Cassandra approached the pedestal, she was shocked to find Jacquelyn stepping off to leave. Cassandra had no idea Jacquelyn was also engaged, and it was unbearable to see her wearing a jeweled designer gown from the expensive rack. The dress was cut low in the back with a sweetheart neckline in front, trimmed with shimmering beads, accentuating Jacquelyn's beautiful body. To Cassandra, everything about her was the way a bride should look—captivating, dazzling, and seductive.

"How stupid I am. Jason would love a gown like that—not some old dumpy thing I just picked out." Cassandra returned to the fitting room, devastated. She pulled the dress off before Daphne and Sophia saw her in it, insisting they go at once.

Settling into the Victorian, Daphne told Cassandra about her conversation at the bridal shop. She learned Jacquelyn was getting married in England to Miles Goode. He was hired to produce a show in London where she would be starring as lead actress and singer. Cassandra said very little, moping rather than enjoying this special time in her own life. Daphne went to the kitchen for a plate of chocolates.

"What does this image mean?" Cassandra asked, sounding blasé as she reached for one.

"It's a spiral, representing the cycles of life. For you, it could be a new beginning." Daphne remembered the day Gwen stopped by. "Cassandra, Sophia, come with me to the attic—there's something I want to look for."

"I'm terrified of your staircase after what happened to me last summer," Cassandra resisted.

"What are you talking about?"

"I was scared away by horrible, rumbling noises in the walls. I don't know if I'm willing to try again."

"Noises?"

"You weren't there. You left a note for us to go to the turret by ourselves."

"Hmm," Daphne murmured, recalling a class Arthur held without her. "I can assure you, no unusual noises have happened in my house for a long time. It's up to you—come with me or not," she said, placing her foot on the first step.

Cassandra conceded, taking Sophia's hand to follow behind. Only the creaking of wood under their feet could be heard. They entered the attic together.

"Where's the trunk—where's the trunk?" Daphne repeated to herself, pushing aside carton after carton of belongings tossed about over the years. Dust flew up, and she swatted at thick air. Upon pulling away one final box, she saw the old steamer trunk. Daphne lifted its heavy lid and peered inside, while Sophia and Cassandra looked on with interest.

"Whoever owned this trunk was a seamstress, like my mother," Cassandra commented, seeing fabric and sewing tools on top. She wiped back tears, feeling as though her mother was with her. Daphne stepped aside for Cassandra to dig deeper. When she reached the very bottom of the trunk, she took a breath before pulling out the most beautiful, hand sewn, ivory, silk wedding gown she'd ever seen. Austrian crystals were intricately stitched throughout the bodice. "Is there a mirror here?" Cassandra asked with excitement.

Daphne opened the turret door, and Cassandra walked right through it. Standing before the huge mirror, she held the gown in front of her. "This is the one! This is my dress!" Cassandra glowed in radiant beauty. Then it dawned on her—she was in the turret.

"May I wear it for my wedding?" she asked, rushing back to Daphne and Sophia.

Daphne agreed to let her.

"Cassandra," Sophia said, "I'm afraid this dress won't fit you; it's too small. Victorian women cinched their waists with corsets," she politely added, feeling miserable for stepping on her fantasy.

But unlike Cassandra's usual knee-jerk, defensive reaction, she confidently turned to Sophia. "This dress will fit me and I know exactly how to make it happen," she told her. "And look, there's enough material to let down the hem."

Cassandra carefully placed the dress into the trunk. "Thank you ladies for a great time," she said, merrily running down the stairs. Sophia followed to kiss her goodbye, relieved the day turned out well, in spite of things.

§ § §

Daphne remained in the attic. She lifted the gown from the trunk. Her fingers fondled the crystals, as though she had sewn them onto the garment herself. She carried the dress into the turret and held it up to look in the mirror—then spun around like a young, happy bride.

Friday, March 13
I am feeling a force within me, as if a delicate flower that pushes through a crack in a city sidewalk. ~D~

CHAPTER 32

The Sea Captain

ARLY SPRING MELTED away every trace of snow. Amelia and Thad welcomed Jason and his crew on their first day of work. They anticipated it would take only nine months to get the main house up and running as a Bed and Breakfast. Amelia listed their cottage for sale, hoping to generate additional money for the renovations. Thad attended training seminars to become an innkeeper, keeping his business dealings on hold. But things didn't go as planned. One catastrophe after another held up construction, turning the project into a costly endeavor.

"We're going to have to rip up all the floor boards in the dining room," Jason announced, finding extensive dry rot. "If you want to replace them with matching wood, I'll get you a separate estimate for wide planked fir."

"Okay, okay," Thad agreed, reluctantly. The constant setbacks were taking an emotional, not to mention financial toll on him. He was panicky the cottage had not yet sold, and bills were coming due. "Jason, we might need to rent rooms sooner than we thought. Amelia and I can pry up flooring. You work upstairs and finish the bedrooms and baths."

Jason brought two of his men to the second floor to plaster and prime the walls. He removed years of peeling paint off wide moldings around windows and doors. Taking a break, he admired the coastline. "Look at this view. My fiancée would love a setting like this," he said to the workers. "I gotta get rich to provide something like it."

"Yeah, good luck. Let me know when it happens," one man responded.

§ § §

"Knock, knock, anyone home?" Daphne, Gwen, and Charles said in unison, standing at the front door.

Feeling frazzled, Amelia's mood lightened by their unexpected visit. She was enthused to show off the progress. It didn't seem as bad after hearing their encouraging words.

"It's looking good, Amelia. I understand what you're going through," Charles offered. He wandered to an adjoining sitting room and ran his hand across the heavy, oak fireplace mantle with fluted side columns. In the center, a replica of a sailing ship was carved in relief, with depictions of moon phases on both sides. He abruptly stepped back, but his eyes remained fixed on the mantle.

Daphne saw his reaction and moved closer. "Beautiful craftsmanship," she spoke.

"I know this ship...I know this ship," Charles choked up. "I have pictures of it in the lobby of my Inn."

Daphne studied the mantle. "You're right. Why is the likeness of the Port Empress ship in this house? Let it be for now. We'll figure it out later."

Lost for words, Charles shook his head and paced the entire downstairs of the house, as if he had been there before. He excused himself, saying he wanted to explore the property. Daphne said good bye to Amelia and followed Charles to the waterfront. He scrutinized the shoreline, eyes searching, stomping back and forth, kicking gritty muck to dislodge wet clumps of sand. He fell to his knees and began digging with his hands like a madman.

Charles got up and ran to another section of the beach. He feverishly pulled away dense vegetation around large boulders. On one in particular, he scraped off algae and encrusted growth with his car keys. He ran his fingers over the cleared surface. "I bought the wrong property!" he wailed.

Daphne was stunned. What would make Charles think he bought the wrong property? She knew he had a deep connection to Franklin Port and needed to reconcile something relating to it, but what significance could there be in a boulder? Charles was deteriorating before Daphne's eyes. He began frantically beating on the huge rock with his fists. Hoping to keep him from slipping into the netherworld of his crazy thoughts again, she decided it best to intervene by suggesting they go back to her house. The sound of her voice was enough to snap him out of it, and they left together.

Charles was not the only one triggered by the carvings on the fireplace mantle. Images began coming to Gwen in rapid succession, much like one of the stories she was preparing for her first fundraiser. She hastily said goodbye to the Fultons, eager to get home and add new information to her narrative.

§ § §

A few hours of daylight remained for Thad and Amelia to continue ripping up floorboards. "What's this?" Thad spoke loudly, referring to something exposed when a corner board was released.

"It looks like folded parchment." Amelia was happy to have a relic from a previous owner. She carefully pulled it out and opened it, while Thad continued removing nails.

"Oh my, what have we here?" Amelia was shining a flashlight on the fragile document.

Thad stopped working and looked at Amelia's ashen face. The parchment had a hand-drawn map with a written message she read aloud.

June 12, 1863

It is not without considerable guilt that I write about my transgression. I ask to be judged by the good and honest service I have performed over my lifetime rather than by this unfortunate lapse of sensibilities. On September 15th, 1862, my crew and I captured the blockade-runner, Moon Tide. We seized and dispersed the cargo except for $500,000 in gold coins I hid in my quarters. I have taken the liberty of bringing the fortune to my own residence in Franklin Port, but my conscience does not allow me to spend it. The gold lies buried on this property. It remains to be found and wisely used for a noble cause. Might this mitigate my torment.

Captain Thomas V. Willington

"This is a treasure map!" Amelia shouted, euphorically. She could barely contain herself, but it was late, and nothing more could be accomplished until morning. "What if there really is buried treasure?" she asked on the ride home, studying the map with a flashlight.

"Don't get your hopes up," Thad responded in a droning voice. "Let's eat dinner and get some sleep. We'll be back tomorrow."

But sleep was not to be had for Amelia, tossing and turning in bed. She thought of all they could do with lots of money—pay off Ivan's tuition, finish the renovation, and lavishly decorate. She snoozed on the living room couch, dreaming her dreams without constraints of waking reality.

CHAPTER 33

Dream Worlds

I T WAS THE first day of spring and, rain or shine, Cassandra always prepped her garden in the Hidden Arbor Cemetery. Months before, Jason agreed to help her, but now felt pressured to finish his job with the Fultons. Caught in a dilemma, he phoned Amelia, and much to his surprise, he was given the morning off.

Cassandra stood outside the bungalow with her duffle bag of tools, anxious to show Jason the patch of land where she sowed seeds each year. He picked her up, and in no time they drove through the cemetery's iron gates. Jason ignored the sight of graves as he stepped out of his truck.

"Hey Gus," Cassandra greeted the smiling groundskeeper. "I'm back."

"Cassandra, look at you. You have a helper—huh?"

"Yes, this is Jason. We're getting married," she blushed.

Gus looked over Cassandra's handsome friend as her father might have. He nodded his approval before dashing away to finish tending the grounds. Jason followed Cassandra to the field, carrying her duffle bag. Without beautiful flowers and vegetables popping from every stem and stalk, the much talked-about garden looked pathetic.

"Gees…we're in a damn cemetery," Jason commented.

"You already knew that."

"Yeah, but standing here with dead people down the road gives it a whole new meaning." He saw Cassandra getting upset. "Hey, what the heck, let's get to work." Jason rolled up his shirtsleeves.

For a good hour, Cassandra raked the hard earth while Jason pulled weeds. "You haven't said a word. What are you thinking about?" she fretted, assuming he was less than thrilled.

"Not much," he answered. Jason couldn't tell her what he really thought about food grown in a cemetery.

Hoping to pique his interest, Cassandra mentioned an historical homestead obscured by the tangle of bramble and briar adjacent to the garden.

"Gus told me about an arbor in there and even a farmhouse. Maybe we can make a path and find them."

Jason looked toward the dark thicket. "Make a path? The vines are small tree trunks. The arbor and house should stay buried." He continued weeding, thinking he was around more old houses lately than he cared to remember.

Taking advantage of Jason's sense of adventure, Cassandra prodded him until he broke down. He grabbed an axe from the stone outbuilding and began chopping away. Cassandra tracked behind with her rake. Finally, another hour later, they broke through the thicket. Wiping sweat off their brows and freeing curling vines caught in their hair, they stood awestruck.

"Oh," Cassandra exclaimed. "The homestead is a magical fairyland."

The flora was mysteriously growing ahead of season. An enthralling world of fiddlehead ferns opened up to a carpet of rich, green moss. Blossoming apple trees outlined a vast meadow with spring bulbs poking through tall grass. The legendary arbor stood as a grand arch with clinging buds about to burst into bloom.

Jason was bowled over. "Maybe you're on to something, Cassie."

She threw down her rake and skipped through billowy Queen Anne's lace leading to the arbor, then dropped to the ground and rolled in warm clover with sweet fragrant flowers. Jason joined her, unable to resist an opportunity to hold and kiss her under a canopy of crystal blue sky. When their lips met, it seemed another moment planned by the stars. Earth's welcoming and intoxicating cradle stirred Jason to ask more of Cassandra—but he didn't. His relationship with his future wife must remain different than with girls in the past. He curled his body alongside hers, and they fell into a deep sleep.

Upon waking, Jason's keen eye saw the corner of a pink-tinted stone flush with the ground. Using only his hands, he vigorously peeled off what could have been a century of weeds and moss, revealing a smooth quartz stone spanning the arbor's threshold. Jason felt chills. Chiseled in old fashioned scroll was—WAKE. The name on the portfolio was forever stuck in his mind. "Why am I finding something else to do with a ghost?" he said under his breath, abruptly standing, wanting to leave.

Cassandra opened her eyes and got up to stop him. "Gus told me townspeople held their wedding ceremonies under this arbor. And look behind those towering pines in the distance—there's the farmhouse," she said, squinting.

"From what I can see, the house should be knocked down." His attitude changed after finding the WAKE stone.

Cassandra knew Jason would prefer a private wedding ceremony followed by a big blast barbeque—maybe at Daphne's. But here she was in the ancestral homestead with the love of her life. It was not necessary to mention the ceremony would take place right where they were standing.

"I have to meet the Fultons this afternoon. Let's explore more of this another day, okay?" Jason was happy for a legitimate excuse to go.

They turned to leave, but the opening to the path had closed up. Frantically searching for a way out, Jason wielded his axe with all his strength. His swing was stopped midair by something hard, hidden in the thick brush. He pulled back vines to reveal a grouping of old tombstones, some leaning over, others standing proudly straight. All of them were surrounding an eight-foot high monument. At its top was a large copper circle. The name of the deceased was etched into the wide base.

OLIVIA WAKE
1896—1916
Died in Childbirth

Cassandra stooped to read the smaller headstones. "Henry, Abigail, Eliza, Hazel, Simon. Didn't Dr. Arthur Wake have a brother named Simon?" she asked, recalling gossip amongst Daphne's students.

"Who knows? I have to get to my job. Let's go." Jason furiously chopped a new opening to the path. They put the tools in the stone building, oblivious to Gus watching them.

§§§

Amelia dressed early and shook her husband to get him up. "Jason called, and I gave him the morning off. We have time to ourselves to follow the map before he and his crew arrive in the afternoon."

Thad, the pragmatist, was eager to finish lifting the flooring and was annoyed Amelia allowed his contractor the morning off. A night's sleep further dulled his interest in the prospect of buried treasure, but he quickly threw himself together, complying with her wild goose chase.

"The map doesn't show the old schoolhouse," Amelia noted, studying it while Thad drove them to the site.

"It was probably built later. I think we'll have to depend upon the directions rather than landmarks."

"There's an X, there really IS an X," Amelia giggled. "It's near the shore-line. How will we find the exact spot?"

"Let's wait until we're there," Thad griped, worried more about fall-ing into a financial hole than the silly map.

Once they arrived at the wetlands, Amelia immediately began the search. Thad followed her, complaining under his breath. Shovels in hand, they held the parchment open to align themselves with the compass drawn on the lower left corner, positioning their backs against the root cellar.

"Walk two hundred paces toward the harbor…forty paces left to-ward the jetty. There's no jetty," Amelia groaned, looking around.

"Maybe there was one. We can possibly find footings under the shift-ing sands."

The beach was more expansive than the one in the drawing, as dredging and weather changed its topography considerably. Knowing exactly where to start digging was like finding a needle in a haystack. Thad was losing patience, but eventually, Amelia located what she thought could be the base of an old jetty. "And from here, 20 paces north to a large boulder with a mark on it," she rambled. "Is there a boulder on the property?"

"Look around, there are boulders galore. What kind of a mark does your special one have?" Thad asked with a clenched jaw.

"It's a crescent moon," she responded tersely.

Every boulder was covered with vegetation. After an hour of pacing and scraping, scraping and pacing, Thad had enough and went to work inside the house, leaving Amelia in her dream world.

She was about to give up when she saw what looked like a time-eroded, chiseled impression of a crescent moon on top of one of the boulders. The slimy covering had recently been scraped off. With renewed vigor, she started digging a hole in the sand below the marking. Three feet down, her shovel stopped.

"THAD! THAAADEEEUSS!"

Startled by screams he heard through the open window, Thad rushed outside and watched Amelia plunge the shovel into the hole one more time for him to hear metal against metal—CLUNK. He grabbed his shovel and dug deeper to help unearth whatever was beneath.

There it was—a large chest with thick metal straps. It appeared to have been buried a long time. Thad cleared around it, lowering himself into the trench. He hollowed out the base to leverage the chest up—but it wouldn't budge.

"Should I call for help?" Amelia asked, watching her husband struggling.

"Let's do this on our own," he answered decisively. "It's too heavy to lift. We'll have to empty it. Get the trash can and pry bar from inside," he ordered.

Hurrying back, Amelia handed Thad the tool. "Here goes nothing," he said. With only a few forceful motions, the lid released. Thad's jaw dropped as he slowly opened the trunk. Amelia peered over him to see. The chest was filled to the top with coins—gold coins dating back to mid-1860s, as far as Thad could tell.

His voice deepened. "These are worth a fortune."

"Are you serious?"

"They appear to be real gold. I know people who have sold coins from this era, and they came away with huge sums of money to invest."

"Great fortunes have their own burdens," Amelia sighed, remembering Daphne's teachings.

"What did you say?" Thad sniped. The task of getting the coins into the trash can was weighing on his mind.

"Nothing, I said nothing."

Hastily, Thad passed handful upon handful of coins to Amelia. They were careful not to lose a single one, unaware the tide was quickly rising.

"Hurry up!" Amelia shrieked, seeing a puddle of foam swirling around her feet. Water began pouring into the hole, and its walls started collapsing.

They finished emptying the trunk in the nick of time. The opening completely filled with water up to Thad's waist. He struggled to climb out of what was feeling like a pit of quicksand. Just as Amelia reached for her shovel to help him escape, the strengthening backwash floated it away. "Oh no, now what do we do?"

Thad put his arms up and Amelia pulled, working harder than ever, freeing him from a certain death. With a loud, sucking noise—he was out. Thad and Amelia dragged the heavy pail of coins to their car, leaving the property before Jason arrived to work. The sea rolled in, and shifting sands claimed the chest once more.

CHAPTER 34

A Good Friend

CASSANDRA WAS CONVINCED her August wedding must take place under the arbor. She was also determined to fit into the gorgeous gown in Daphne's attic. Although she didn't know for sure how either might happen, she created a plan including both.

Cassandra went directly to the homestead each day after work. Pruning tools in hand, she cut back the thicket's brush, motivating herself to stick with the daunting task by visualizing the wedding dress. She diligently worked until early evening. As her waist began to shrink, she paid more attention to diet. Even better, she let go of jealous thoughts. The memory of Jacquelyn in the bridal salon became her inspiration, rather than her envy. The future was her choice.

§ § §

"Care to explain where you're going?" Gus inquired, seeing her heading in the direction of the homestead one Saturday morning.

"Oh," Cassandra flushed at being caught. "I thought since no one uses the property, Jason and I might be married under the arbor," she openly admitted, biting her nails at the possibility she overstepped her bounds. "I guess I should have asked for permission," she sulked.

"Nonsense, Cassandra—the arbor has been waiting for you." His voice echoed across the gravestones. "I'll tell you what. As my wedding gift, I can help out by working evenings after you leave."

"Oh thank you. You can't imagine how much this means to me."

"I think you have it wrong—it's how much it means to me."

Cassandra returned Sunday morning. Her head reeled over seeing what Gus accomplished in one night. He finished everything she started. The morning air was cool. Cassandra walked through the thicket. The earth below her feet seemed to drink up the rising sun, perhaps for the first time in decades.

Standing at the end of the path, she could see the entire homestead.

Missing pieces of wooden lattice on the arbor were replaced and painted. The smooth stone underneath it appeared polished, emitting rays of light, highlighting WAKE. Beyond the towering pines, even the farmhouse had a fresh coat of paint, and its windows were framed with new black shutters. The tall, unruly grass in the meadow was trimmed to an emerald lawn, extending as far as the eye could see. There was nothing left to do.

So confounded by the miracles abounding, Cassandra didn't hear Jason calling her. "There you are. I stopped by the bungalow to take you to breakfast. Something told me to come here," he said, taking a look around. "Who did all this? It's spectacular." He didn't care about her answer because he was now looking at her. His bride-to-be also transformed. "You look spectacular."

No finer words could have been spoken. More self-assured, Cassandra asked if they could have their ceremony under the arbor.

"This must be private property. How can we get married here?" Jason questioned.

"Gus said it would be okay. He prepared it for us."

Jason acquiesced. He led her under the arbor, just to try it out.

§ § §

In the summer heat, Gus watered Cassandra's magical dream world every evening, but by day, they were like two ships passing in the night. Only the smell of pipe tobacco lingering in the air indicated Gus was close at hand.

While Jason juggled renovations at the Port Empress Inn, Thad also asked him to move things along with his property. Jason assumed Thad and Amelia sold their cottage to pay for extra men on the job. In time for the summer season, the Fulton's project was complete, and so was the Inn—all to Jason's credit.

Franklin Port's vibrant tourist season was underway. Daphne held her Fourth of July gala, but fewer people attended. Even the phantom schooner and its captain did not show up. Daphne took it as a sign the sadness must have lifted, and so the gathering should be her last.

New things were on the horizon for Daphne's star students. Amelia's Moon Tide Bed and Breakfast was about to hold its grand opening. Gwen's first fundraiser for the Historical Society was scheduled for midsummer. And of course, Cassandra's wedding would be in August.

CHAPTER 35

Flashing Insight

THE REGION EXPERIENCED the hottest temperatures on record. People grew lazy, passing spare time on porches sipping cool drinks. Children played under sprinklers spouting cold water during the day, while at night television sets could be heard through open, screened windows. Most everyone avoided expending extra effort, but not Daphne's trio of former students.

Amelia and Thad agreed to host the Historical Society's fundraising event on the last Saturday in July. It was to feature Gwen's storytelling. The old school on the property was converted to a lecture hall and marine study center, and the house was a popular Bed and Breakfast. Town curiosity was at an all-time high over the extravagant renovation. Not since the days of Simon Wake, so long ago, and then Daphne's Victorian, had there been such gossip about a personal undertaking. As a result, every one of the hundred tickets sold.

Ladies arrived dressed in long, flowing skirts and brimmed sunhats. Men sported the requisite madras shirts or Bermuda shorts. Daphne wore a powder-blue frou frou dress. She and Charles had become closer during recent months, but kept their relationship private enough for busybodies to speculate.

Cocktails and hors d'oeuvres were served under a white canvas tent erected halfway between the house and the water's edge. People strolled across the grounds and toured the buildings.

"This must be costing the Historical Society a fortune," Charles remarked to Daphne, while biting into a succulent shrimp.

"Amelia told me she and Thad paid the expenses out of pocket, so ticket sales would fully benefit the society."

"Where did they get the money? When we were here a few months ago, Thad was stressed about finances. Even if they sold their cottage, the numbers don't add up," Charles pondered out loud.

Daphne knew the Fulton's cottage hadn't sold. It did seem odd Amelia and Thad restored both buildings with exquisite taste and now funded the affair. Amelia darted around making sure everyone was having a good time, but when she walked up to Charles, something outlandish came over her.

"I'm happy to see you, Captain." She wrapped her hands around his face to pull it closer and kiss him on the lips.

"Hannah—how improper for a lady in public," Charles chastised, pushing her hands away. Amelia headed toward another guest as though nothing unusual happened, but Charles couldn't shake off what just transpired. "Why did she call me Captain and kiss me on the lips? Why did I call her Hannah?" he asked Daphne.

"I don't know why. It baffled me too."

The crowd gathered inside the house to hear Gwen's talk. By the time Daphne and Charles left the lawn, the only seats remaining were along the back wall by the tall, dining room windows.

Lillian, head of the Historical Society, addressed the guests. "Welcome everybody to the Moon Tide on this hot, summer afternoon."

The words Moon Tide jarred Charles.

"I would like to thank our gracious hosts, Amelia and Thad Fulton," Lillian announced.

There was thunderous applause. Charles put his hands over his ears—it was too loud, reminding him of the night when the Port Empress Inn came alive with ghosts. He turned his head away from the speaker and gazed at the shoreline.

"I think you're in for a special treat," Lillian continued. "It is my pleasure to introduce Gwen Davens. Gwen is known as a gifted psychic."

"A psychic, are you kidding?" someone heckled. "I came to hear town history."

"Ladies and gentlemen, please withhold your judgment so we can enjoy the narrative. I promise you it will be entertaining."

"Then get on with it," a shrill voice shouted.

"Gwen has taken the historical record of the sunken ship Port Empress and given the saga richness to touch your spirit. Gwen, it's all yours." Lillian walked away from the podium.

Those words, Port Empress, sunken ship, richness, and spirit ripped through Charles, even though the history faced him every day on the walls of his Inn. He felt he was slipping into his netherworld.

Gwen nervously greeted the crowd. She began her fascinating account of the infamous ship, Port Empress, sinking with hundreds of soldiers returning after the Civil War. In riveting detail, she described the stormy weather, strong tide, and horrified crowd watching on land. Charles was further agitated by her yarn. Then Gwen spoke of one mourner in particular, Hannah Willington, the wife of the ship's captain.

"Charles, you called Amelia Hannah," Daphne stated in a hushed voice. "And Willington is the family name on my mother's side. I had a great, great grandmother named Hannah Willington!"

Charles was listening to Daphne while also hearing Gwen. Two stories were being interwoven with his own life. It was as though streamers from a Maypole were becoming entwined, and he was unable to break free from the entanglement. His heart beat faster.

"Mrs. Willington was devastated by more than the death of her husband," Gwen told her audience. "Without his income, she and her five children fell upon desperate times. However, she knew a secret that could have eased their lives, but it never came to pass."

Gwen heightened the suspense with subtle, theatrical nuances in her voice. She was perfect for her new job.

"Tragically, when her husband perished on the Port Empress, he took with him knowledge of the location of what in today's equivalent would be millions of dollars in gold coins. They were stolen from a blockade runner and then buried by her husband—somewhere—right along this very shoreline. Hannah knew about the gold, but not where it was buried. Men and their secrets," Gwen muttered to herself, forgetting she was holding a microphone.

The women chuckled. Some listeners were on edge, but none more than Amelia and Thad. Gwen started rubbing her eyes—a new flash of insight was coming, not part of her original lecture.

"But...but," she stammered over her words. "The gold has been found—on this property—and recently." Gwen turned to look at Amelia and Thad, placing a hand over her mouth to stop the outpouring of information.

The crowd buzzed. Everyone was suspicious where the money came from to refurbish the Fulton place in such a bang-up way—and so quickly. Even Jason wondered after having been paid handsomely for his work.

Amelia poked Thad's arm. "Say something. Gwen knows everything."

"Shush, Amelia, that's not possible. How could she know everything?"

"I don't have time to explain, just stand up and speak to them."

Thad broke into a sweat and hesitantly stepped to the front of the room.

He never expected the public to find out about the gold. All eyes were now on him. "May I provide an ending to your story, Gwen?" Thad asked, realizing he had no choice.

Relieved of having to divulge anything more, Gwen agreed.

Thad began. "When I was pulling up floorboards, I found an old letter with a map leading to buried treasure on this land. Gwen, in fact, your psychic vision is completely accurate."

The audience reacted—some people fidgeted in their seats. The event was supposed to be an entertaining presentation. No one ever anticipated such a revelation. Daphne turned to speak to Charles, but his seat was empty. She had been so absorbed by the story that she missed seeing him open the window and climb outside. He was standing by the water.

"The map led us to a huge boulder on the beach. And sure enough, there was a buried chest of gold coins," Thad added.

"The money doesn't belong to you any more than it did to the thief who stole it," a jealous neighbor called out.

"Where's the money now?" an angry woman asked. "Did you squander it on these ritzy buildings?"

"The money belongs to the town," a man demanded of Thad.

Gwen was beside herself for creating such turmoil for her friends. The energy in the room turned even more hostile. Thad and Amelia were frightened. A woman, who sat silently in the irate crowd, rose to her feet and introduced herself.

"My name is Bonnie Baylen. I'm here as a guest of the Fultons, but I'm also executive director of the County Foundation for Preservation of Waterways. We assist communities like yours in maintaining and protecting their waters and shorelines. Without our programs, much of your recreational and fishing industries would be at risk. I'm pleased to inform you that the Fultons properly researched the legalities of the treasure, paid the taxes, and donated a considerable endowment to the Foundation."

The audience didn't know how to respond. They couldn't dispute an honorable deed. Everyone quieted.

"This donation will benefit coastal residents, including you and your loved ones, for years to come," the spokeswoman finished.

Daphne could see Charles leaning against a boulder. He appeared to be crying. The converging information now made sense to her. While the audience's attention was still glued to the podium, she also climbed out the window and ran to him.

"Charles, it's okay, it's all over—I finally understand your crazy thoughts. In another lifetime, you were Captain Willington of the sunken ship Port Empress, but you are my wonderful Charles Hinds in this one. Let the guilt of your past life go—it no longer serves you. The stolen money has been donated to a good cause, and maybe it was meant for that purpose from the beginning. Perhaps we are only actors on a stage, performing in a grand plan that goes around and around until all things correct themselves."

Charles struggled to understand what she was saying. "If you are a descendent of the Willington family in this life, are we related?"

Daphne laughed and held both his hands. "Oh no, not at all—we return to this world sometimes into the same bloodline, sometimes a different one, but nevertheless, it's another chance to get it right."

Charles breathed a sigh of relief. Whatever had been tormenting him all these years was laid to rest by the charity of the Fultons.

"Let's go inside and congratulate our friends for such wonderful accomplishments," Daphne coaxed. "Heave ho, Captain Willington!" Great, Great Grandpa, she thought to herself, smiling.

Charles laughed, feeling freer than ever before. No one besides Daphne would know his connection to Captain Willington, if only he was able to keep Gwen from rubbing her eyes in his presence. But unlike buried treasure, his history could never be proven.

Saturday, July 25
Now that Charles is no longer haunted by his past, I fear he won't need me anymore. ~D~

CHAPTER 36

Welcomed Gifts

A THINNER CASSANDRA VISITED Daphne to try on the gown found in the attic trunk. The dress was cleaned and lengthened, looking more beautiful than she remembered. Daphne held it over Cassandra's head. Like a fine fitting glove, it slipped down her slender body with ease. The tiny silk buttons along the back closed perfectly.

"Wow…you set an intention and succeeded in reaching your goal," Daphne praised.

"Thank you. I couldn't have done it without your teachings."

"I would like to give you and Jason my wedding gift now," Daphne said, unbuttoning the gown for her to change back into her clothes. When Cassandra was ready, she followed Daphne next door to the guesthouse. "Welcome to your new home."

Cassandra flushed with excitement. "Am I going to live here?"

Daphne took her hand and they went inside the beautifully furnished, two-bedroom dwelling. It smelled of lavender and fresh lemons. The walls were white painted bead board, and the waxed, wooden floors gleamed where the sun filtered in. The couch and chairs in the main room had crisp, fitted slipcovers of blue and white ticking. A bouquet of flowers sat atop the mantle of the stone fireplace. Cassandra closed her eyes in disbelief upon the sight of a huge bathtub, like the one in her childhood farmhouse. "I feel I belong here," she told Daphne.

Daphne led Cassandra to the expansive backyard. "There's one more thing. You're welcome to plant your garden on the property. The soil is rich and the view can't be beat. I hope you and Jason will be happy here for as long as you want to stay. You can save money and someday buy the house of your dreams."

Cassandra remembered the first time she walked past Daphne's Victorian, and it was the house of her dreams. She hugged Daphne and said she couldn't wait to share the news of the extraordinary wedding present with Jason.

Daphne still had something else on her mind. "Jason told me about your plans for the wedding. Is it true it's going to be in the Hidden Arbor Cemetery? Everyone has put the date aside, but we're waiting for the final decision as to where it will take place. Please…tell me you're joking."

"I don't know why I'm set on having the ceremony at the old homestead, but I think it will be dreamy, trust me."

"Child, you're sounding like me. I won't argue. By the way, as his contribution, Charles offered to manage and cater the event at the Port Empress Inn—or the cemetery."

Cassandra was over the moon and headed to her bungalow. She began ruminating on the absence of her mother during this special time. If her mother was still alive, the wedding would bring joy to her hard life.

Amigo greeted Cassandra at the door, wagging his tail. The main room became cold for no apparent reason. She closed the windows, but the chill persisted. Amigo began clawing at a wooden box serving as an end table. This was unusual behavior for him, prompting Cassandra to look inside. The box contained items from her family home, hurriedly salvaged when she moved under duress. She felt grounded enough to examine them and tentatively removed everything.

Cassandra sorted through old letters, wrapped mementos, and eventually came across a service medal bearing her father's name. Holding it to the sunlight, she read aloud an official paper citing his bravery during the war. Even more moving was the letter from her father to her mother.

My Dearest Gloria,

You'll never know the misery of war or the depths of pain I carried home to you and our children. But you continuously stood by me, for better and for worse. You'll always be the hero in my eyes. I write these words to you should I never speak them before my death.

Love,
Warren

Cassandra sat on the floor holding the precious letter on her lap and sobbed. She realized how these unspoken expressions of love and compassion might have healed broken hearts and made sense of unfulfilled promises. But the past was the past—she couldn't fix it. She had to lay her anger and sadness to rest in order to be swept up by the joy in her own life.

Cassandra drove to the homestead to prune the prolific blooms and greenery with Amigo faithfully leading the way along the widened path through the thicket. She was surprised at how dry everything was. The plants around the arbor drooped, the lawn browned. She wondered why Gus stopped watering for her in the heat. Cassandra feared her wedding plans would fall apart.

The distance from the garden well was too great to hook up a hose. Buckets were also out of the question. She assumed Gus was using another well by the old farmhouse. Cassandra walked toward the eerie structure, feeling apprehensive. This was the first time she had been so close to the off-putting pines guarding it, but desperate to save the vegetation from withering further, she searched the grounds. There was no source of water to be found.

Amigo darted off behind a patch of shrubs. Cassandra found him lying by an upright limestone slab. The gravesite was free from years of moss and weeds, as if recently cleared. Cassandra froze when she read it, struggling to comprehend what was before her.

Gustav Holm

Gus

1822 — 1892

Good Friend

Devoted Groundskeeper

"Gus—this is Gus—I don't understand." Tears streamed down her cheeks. "Amigo, come," she called, eager to rush home. She wanted to contact Gwen to meet her at the cemetery before dark, believing Gwen's psychic abilities would make sense of the gravestone.

§ § §

Keeping her appointment with Cassandra, Gwen left her house just as a spontaneous breeze picked up. An uncanny drop in temperature accompanied dark clouds rolling in. Seeing the blackened sky, Gwen remembered this exact set of circumstances last summer when she found Cassandra in the cemetery. Gwen drove through the iron gates and down the road.

She jammed on her brakes to avoid hitting a man she saw in sepia vision, presuming him to be the same one as before. This time, he was wearing a white medical coat, like the figure in the turret racing to save a boy in the water. She was convinced he was the ghost of Dr. Arthur Wake. He waved for Gwen to follow to a distant corner in the graveyard. She parked and walked behind him. He stopped next to a flat, carved stone in the earth for her to read.

Baby Gracie Ann Davens
Born and died December 24, 1916

The air went out of Gwen. She kneeled in the grass and stroked the tiny grave marker of the twin sister she never knew about. Although ripped apart at birth, a bond had formed in the womb and remained unbroken.

After so many years, it all became clear to Gwen. Her loving sister, whose spirit stayed with her, was mistaken for Gwen in her childhood. It was her sister's name on the wedding invitations, deeply upsetting her mother. In Gwen's dreams, her twin was at the other end of the cord, and also appeared in the center of the dance circle. She was her double in the turret's mirror. Gracie Ann was part of the in-between-space from where Gwen's sepia visions came. An amber haze rolled in like a fog off the harbor, and Gwen was shown the story of her birth.

1916—Arthur put down the pen. He wrote all he could to his estranged brother, Simon. It was difficult for him to invite his brother to Christmas dinner the next day, but Olivia was expecting their baby in a few weeks, and making amends with Simon was her greatest desire.

Arthur left the letter on the desk and went into the kitchen to eat breakfast with his wife. The telephone rang in his office. There was urgency in his voice as he hurried past Olivia on his way out of the house. Helen Davens was a nervous woman and thought she was in labor. He rushed to her home, assuming it was just another false alarm—but he was wrong.

Mrs. Davens was in hard labor and the birth was imminent. Dr. Wake arrived not a minute too soon when the particularly tiny baby slipped out into his hands. He wrapped the infant girl in swaddling clothes and summoned the father, when the new mother began screaming. There was an unexpected second infant emerging, but the contractions weakened. The baby was born with the cord tightly around her neck—she never took a breath.

Dr. Wake blamed himself for missing the second heartbeat. The scene of grieving parents overwhelmed him. He wondered how he could ever be forgiven. Arthur prepared the paperwork for Gwendolyn and Gracie Ann Davens and left to drown his guilt at a pub outside of town where he would not be recognized. He ignored his promise to Olivia to come home early because he didn't have the strength to face Simon.

When he finally made it home, police officers were in front of the Victorian. Arthur rushed to them, fear coursing through him. Given the news of Olivia's death, he felt as if his heart stopped, and he was floating out of his body. The officers' voices were muffled and distant. Nothing seemed real. The police escorted him into his house where Simon was sitting by the Christmas tree, holding the infant boy.

"Arthur, where were you? For crying out loud, if you had only come home, this would not have happened. You could have saved her...you could have..."

Simon's voice trailed off into tears of sorrow. Nothing could be undone, none of it. Arthur glanced over at his Christmas gift for Olivia lying under the tree, wrapped in shiny red and green paper. It was a beautifully framed portrait of his wife. Through the wrapping, he could visualize Olivia's chignon held in place by the diamond hair clip he gave her on their wedding day. The painting was all he had left.

Simon offered the baby for Arthur to hold. Instead, Arthur turned his back and climbed the stairs for bed. He was a broken man.

The sky opened up and a torrential rain drenched Gwen to the bone. Thunder and lightning jolted her to the present. She erupted into tears. The magnitude of what she saw seeped into her psyche. Unanswered questions ceased, she now had the gift the ghost promised—knowing about her sister. She stood up and looked directly at the hazy outline of the ghost.

"I'm sorry for your pain and sadness. You were not to blame—you were a good doctor, assisting my mother, rather than being with your wife. You did everything you could," she softly spoke.

Dr. Arthur Wake's worldly existence needed that closure. He lowered his eyes in appreciation of her forgiveness and then disappeared.

Forgetting she was meeting Cassandra, Gwen got into the car to leave just as Cassandra parked next to her. Gwen motioned they would have to speak to each other at another time. She sped off.

Cassandra waved goodbye and stepped out into the welcomed rain. Here was yet another gift—this time from Mother Nature.

CHAPTER 37

Getting Even

ALTHOUGH JASON WAS a good, solid man, Cassandra was concerned when his friends planned a bachelor party for him. Jason had a natural spontaneity, not always well thought out. He was also stubborn when his freedom was impinged upon, and Cassandra knew, as his future wife, it would be a balancing act for her. "Will Fred be there?" she asked.

Jason kissed her on the lips, managing to alleviate her fears by reciting the list of married and responsible men throwing the party. All of what he said was true, while avoiding her question. Fred, unlike Jason's other buddies, would cast caution to the wind. He was a hard-laboring welder by day, but after hours he liked to play without worrying about repercussions. As Jason left Cassandra's bungalow, he swore he would behave.

The men attending the party gathered at the Franklin Port Grille on the outskirts of town. It was frequented by mellow dinner crowds who raved about good food and house-brewed beer on tap. Later at night, artsy types following a theatre performance as well as rebellious bikers and their women hung out, listening to music.

After hours of celebration, most of the married men in Jason's group were ready to return to their families, while Fred kept the party going for those who stayed. Jason was careful to avoid getting drunk and finding himself in a less than noble predicament, as happened before. He went to the phone booth several times to call Cassandra and reassure her he was not drinking heavily.

"When are you leaving, Jason?" she inquired, reminding him it was already past midnight.

"Cassie, come on, I'm still with my buddies, and I only had two beers."

Cassandra wanted to believe him, but doubt had a louder voice. "Sure, I bet your buddies are all being perfect gentlemen and ignoring the girls at the bar, huh Jason?"

"Gees, Cassandra. I'll call you when I get home." He hung up—unhappy she was trying to control him. When Jason returned to the bar, a group came in for a drink after a show. In the midst of them was Jason's ultimate, forbidden temptation—Jacquelyn. He stared at her, and she quickly ushered her friends to a table in the far corner.

"This is your last chance to have some fun as a free man," Fred egged his buddy on, noticing something brewing between him and the woman.

Ignoring Fred, Jason turned his back to Jacquelyn and concentrated on blowing smoke rings. An hour later, Jacquelyn's friends left, but she didn't go with them. Instead, she went to the ladies room. Fred stood outside its door after waiting all night to stir something up for Jason. When Jacquelyn came face to face with Fred, he was thrown for a loop—she was a knock out.

Nearing the witching hour, it was predominantly a man's world in the Franklin Port Grille. Personalities were unrestrained by alcohol. That suited Fred perfectly. He was a confirmed bachelor, always on the prowl, and never interested in a woman after he conquered his prize. He blocked Jacquelyn, refusing to let her pass. She stepped to one side, and he did the same. She liked the game, checking to be sure Jason was watching, hoping to make him jealous. Fred was good looking, muscular, and cocky—like he owned the world. Jacquelyn loved teasing such men, but on that night she teased the wrong one.

Fred never took no for an answer, especially after a woman led him to believe she was interested. When Jacquelyn realized she had taken her playfulness too far, she pushed Fred aside to get by. There were heated words between them, but the men at the bar, mostly bikers, ignored the conflict. She was on her own.

Jason watched. Jacquelyn's raw audacity fascinated him just as it did the night at the Port Empress Inn. Only after Fred hustled her, did Jason intervene, shoving Fred against a table. Fred sprang back, ready to fight. Jacquelyn laughed, fueling the fire between the men, but finally, they managed to cool down.

Jason put his jacket over Jacquelyn's shoulders and escorted her outside. This time—he held her closely. "Where's your car?" he asked.

"It's parked behind the theatre."

"Did you deliberately miss your ride?"

She didn't answer.

Jason was in a quandary, struggling with his decision to get Jacquelyn safely to her vehicle. As she climbed into his truck, he stared at her long, naked legs and again questioned whether he made the best choice for a wife. Turning the ignition key, his headlights shined directly into the smoky bar windows. He could see Gus watching him, but had no idea when he arrived. Jason feared Cassandra would find out he was with Jacquelyn.

The voice of reason was in Jason's head, but he was awash with quite something else. He didn't know which would win out. Wanting Gus to think he had integrity, he went inside to offer him a ride too, but Gus was gone. Jason returned to his truck where Jacquelyn sat impatiently, ready to play the cards in her hand.

"Do you remember how you left me the other time?" she challenged, referring to the escapade at the Port Empress Inn last winter.

"I tried calling, and you hung up on me—your guilt trip isn't going to work," Jason argued, feeling as though he had been set up. He backed his truck away from the bar and sped off, trying to sound nonchalant, although his emotions were churning.

"Why don't we go to the beach to talk?" Jacquelyn proposed sweetly, refusing to let his indifference get in the way. This was her last chance to be with Jason as both their lives were rapidly going in different directions. While he drove, she studied his profile.

He was drop-dead handsome, but was probably flat broke and had none of the sophistication she found in Miles.

Jacquelyn questioned what it was about Jason that attracted her. She remembered riding old fashioned carousels when she was younger. Painted wooden animals moved around a mirrored calliope. Riders reached over to a machine dispensing metal rings—but only one ring was golden. If someone was lucky enough to grab it, a prize was given. In Jacquelyn's mind, Cassandra got the golden ring, and Jason was the prize. That drove her nuts.

Truth be told, Jacquelyn could never love a man such as Jason. Miles was a better fit for her. She would have glamour, excitement, and all the best parts on stage. But on that night, only one thing mattered—Jacquelyn had a score to settle with Jason.

Jason saw her twisting a diamond ring on her finger. "Is that an engagement ring?" he asked, falling into her trap. "I didn't know you were getting married."

"Didn't your fiancée tell you?"

Jason refused to respond. His truck was heading toward the fork in the road leading to either the beach or her car parked behind the theatre. The direction he chose would influence the rest of his life. Jacquelyn looked out her window, sighed, and crossed her legs to hike her short skirt higher. She could feel his eyes on her tanned, silky skin. Jason gripped the steering wheel tighter. He didn't want to begin a conversation, as there were too many unspoken feelings between them. If Jason was honest with himself, he liked the contrasts in Jacquelyn, the good, bad, and mostly—the beautiful.

The sign on the road indicated the cut off to the beach was coming up. When Jacquelyn saw it, she knew she had little time left, and since she used up her tactics of guilt and seduction, she played the last card.

"I could have frozen to death on the Inn's porch. I never thanked you for saving my life." She placed her hand on his shoulder, tense from gripping the wheel. "And I also want to thank you for tonight. I could have been...you know...hurt." She ran her hand along his arm before putting it back on her lap.

The fork was just ahead. The truck barreled down the road at full speed...

CHAPTER 38

It's Done!

Saturday, August 15, 1970

A S PROMISED, CHARLES organized Jason and Cassandra's entire wedding, including a moonlight reception at the Port Empress Inn. He wanted the ceremony at the homestead to be just as sensational and surrounded the arbor with a semicircle of ivory-colored chairs. There was little else to do on the property, as it had been meticulously readied. A spectacular bloom of entwined, blue morning glories, oddly open in the heat of late afternoon, stood out against a profusion of white baby's breath enveloping the arbor. Charles placed a white satin runner along the ground, edged with fragrant sweet alyssum.

The guests streamed in for the affair scheduled to begin at six o'clock. They parked their cars and walked along the manicured path to the meadow of lush plantings. The strange juxtaposition of a wedding in a cemetery made some giggle, while others were mortified. Nevertheless, the air was charged with excitement.

Daphne became weak when she saw the arbor. Sophia held her arm and guided her to chairs next to Thad and Amelia. Charles kept looking over at Daphne from where he stood as Jason's best man, understanding her emotions. In the turret, they witnessed another wedding under the same arbor—but through a mirror.

Jason, the epitome of masculine good looks, was dressed in a black tuxedo with a silk vest. Standing near the pastor, he was flanked by Charles and Gwen. Jason nervously waited, never daring to take his eyes off the opening in the thicket, remaining very quiet. The passing minutes were agonizing. By 6:30, the bride had not shown up. Even though Jason struggled with second thoughts about marrying Cassandra, he was now certain she was the right woman for him. He worried Gus may have said something to change her mind.

There was a higher plan at work. Cassandra's lateness created anticipation, like extended pauses between musical notes, causing the listener to yearn for resolution. Jason looked increasingly uneasy. He was unaware the Invisible orchestrated a delay in the wedding. Magic was about to manifest.

The air was hushed until, finally, Amigo dashed down the white runner to greet Jason with gusto, providing comic relief. Everyone broke into laughter at his antics. One small step at a time, Cassandra came into view, breathtakingly gorgeous. The guests gave an audible sigh at her exquisite transformation. The Victorian wedding gown looked as though it was made for her. Shimmering crystals reflected the sunlight, accentuating her beauty. Cassandra looked the way she dreamed a bride should—captivating, dazzling, and seductive.

Gwen twitched, making every effort to stay in the moment, but the sight of the flowers took her back to the day she had originally seen them in the turret mirror, shown by her double—her sister. She began rubbing her eyes. At once, another vision came.

1967—Gwen saw a saltbox house on a large tract of farmland. Inside, a younger Cassandra was sitting at her mother's deathbed, crying. They were having their final words with one another.

"Mom, please don't die. I'll be alone. Where will I go, what will I do? I'm begging you to live another day."

"Cassie, I'll be with you forever," her mother spoke in a faint, raspy voice.

"How…how will I know you are with me?" Cassandra wept. "I desperately need something to hold on to for the rest of my life—in marriage and as a mother."

With her last ounce of strength, Cassandra's mother barely lifted her hand and placed it over her daughter's. "You'll know, Cassie. Your father and I will travel on the wings of doves and butter…"

"I live on a farm—but—butter?" Cassandra reflected upon her mother's last words.

Gwen's vision disappeared as a guitarist played a haunting wedding song while the bride walked along the satin runner. The guests were so stirred there wasn't a dry eye among them. Cassandra approached the arbor to take her place next to Jason standing upon the Wake family stone. Gwen lifted Cassandra's veil over her upswept honey-colored hair, revealing the diamond studded clip Daphne loaned her. Cassandra's face shone. She was a traditional bride with something old, something new, something borrowed, and something blue—the flowers arching over the arbor.

Cassandra's aura of love extended outward and its embrace could be felt by the entire gathering. It was a poignant moment for Daphne, whose breath became shallow as she held back tears.

"Keep going, Cassandra, keep going," Gwen whispered in her ear when she saw the bride hesitate to stand next to Jason. Cassandra was searching the sky for a sign from her mother.

Cassandra took one more step onto the quartz stone under the arbor, adding her name to memories of nuptials long ago. An ancestral choir of birds, hidden in the enormous pine trees, broke the silence with song. Two doves flew out and soared through the air, leaving behind a ribbon of misty lace. They weaved over guests and landed in the morning glories, remaining there until the vows were complete.

On the ground at the bride's feet, a splendid Monarch butterfly alighted, fluttering its wings and flying into Cassandra's bouquet, to rest for a while. A tear rolled down her cheek. "Butter…a butterfly…thank you, Mommy." Cassandra basked in the supernatural expression of love, hope, and promise. The couple turned to greet their well-wishers for the first time as husband and wife. Both doves lifted into flight, returning to the trees.

Following Amigo and Charles, the crowd headed to the Port Empress Inn for an evening of dining and dancing. Cassandra asked Jason to stay behind. She understood none of what happened since she moved to Franklin Port, especially with the homestead, but knew she needed to thank Gus.

"I have to show you something," she said to Jason, holding his hand. Cassandra led him to Gus's grave on the side of the farmhouse. She was concerned if this phenomenon was known sooner, to anyone, all plans in the homestead would have been canceled.

Jason was astounded. "Cassie, I don't get it. Did Gus just die?"

"No, look at the date. He died a long time ago. Help must be available from the Other Side."

Jason became emotional. He put his arm around his beautiful bride. A gentle breeze carried the sweet, fruity scent of pipe tobacco.

"It's done," Cassandra spoke to her husband, not knowing where the words came from.

Hand in hand, they walked through the thicket and never looked back. The paint on the farmhouse peeled, shutters sagged, greenery browned, and thick vines reclaimed the path. As if a movie winding backwards, the arbor and homestead reverted to their previous state.

CHAPTER 39

But Only for an Instant

SEVERAL MONTHS AFTER the wedding, Cassandra and Jason announced they were going to have a baby. Daphne encouraged Sophia to retire and move into the Victorian to enjoy her son's growing family. The excitement and preparations for the blessed event kept everyone busy right up to the time a boy, Alex, was born in July, 1971.

Alex's birth was touched with poignancy for Daphne. Her daughter, Nancy, gave birth one month later to a beautiful girl, Annabelle Lily. Daphne couldn't be in England to celebrate the occasion. As she watched Alex developing into a toddler, her longing to see Annabelle Lily grew.

When Annabelle was two years old, Nancy brought her to Franklin Port to visit her grandmother. The child, wise beyond her years, squealed with glee at Daphne's whimsical accoutrements on the dining room table. She loved eating chocolate treats and playing in her grandma's castle with Alex, who lived in the guesthouse. Parting with Annabelle Lily and her parents was tearful for Daphne once they returned to England, but she was happy to still have Alex in her life.

The boy was cherubic and good-natured. He did have one little oddity, however. It was a prominent V-shaped birthmark on his right wrist that pointed toward his fingers. His grandmother told him it would bring good luck someday by showing the way to his fortune, like an arrow. Her clever story made Alex less self-conscious.

Cassandra's garden expanded to an impressive size, taking up most of Daphne's backyard and Cassandra's time. Daphne did not object to its overflow as her extravagant parties were a thing of the past, as was so much else. Even with everything going on around her, Daphne's spirit gradually sank, slipping into a melancholic state more profound than ever. She passed time organizing old photographs into scrapbooks, filling in gaps of what went before her near drowning.

Sophia would often return from babysitting Alex to find Daphne curled up in her favorite chair, staring wistfully at a photograph or two.

"Daphne, don't let the past make you so sad. What good does it do?" her friend encouraged.

"It seems everything has come apart. I'm finished with the school, my ghost is gone, my family is overseas, and Charles is planning his future without me. I have let love die over and over. It's created a void, as if a piece of my life is missing. Without understanding what it is, I'm incomplete," Daphne lamented.

"Why do you have to understand? Some things are just a mystifying paradox where what doesn't seem right, is right after all. Why do you need to know all the pieces to feel whole? Love what you have and release the desire for what is not meant to be known. Now, don't I sound like you in your teaching mode?" Sophia laughed nervously.

Daphne looked up, but her attention waned.

"Look at my situation. Who would think I could feel complete after spending decades searching for a man who stole my heart? I have no chance of ever finding Jason's father, so I've let it go. That's what you have to do. This is not like you. Where are your teachings when you need them?"

"And where is my ghost when I need him?" Daphne answered, retreating to the library where she spent afternoons writing in her diary. She seemed to be failing, although nothing threatened her health. It was not anything one could put a finger on—only that her joie de vivre was gone.

§ § §

1974—The morning of Christmas Eve, Daphne sat at the table with Sophia, wrapping last minute gifts. She took the diamond studded hair clip from her pocket, placed it in a lace doily, and tied it with magenta, satin ribbon. She scripted, Annabelle Lily Valentine—I'll always love you, on a shiny, silver gift tag attached to the bow. Daphne placed the present on the fireplace mantle in the dining room.

"Sophia, when I die, it won't be such a tragedy as long as I have a wake," Daphne said offhandedly, as she headed toward the parlor for a nap.

"A wake?" Sophia called after her. "Why are you talking about dying?"

"Oh, Sophia, don't worry so much. It's Christmas Eve. Tonight will be stunning, you'll see," she said, tossing her head back with a soft, girlish giggle.

They were both invited for dinner at the guesthouse. Sophia felt relieved to know Daphne was looking forward to the festivities next door.

By late afternoon, Sophia joined her family while Daphne stayed behind talking to Annabelle on the phone about the special Christmas gift she put aside.

It grew late, and Daphne thought to politely stop in at the guesthouse to give everyone gifts. If Sophia had not been absorbed by Alex's holiday frenzy, she would have noticed her friend was more out of sorts than usual. Not at all hungry, Daphne excused herself soon afterwards to return home.

She organized her table as though holding a class again, placing the brass placard in the center. Entering the turret, she filled the claw foot bathtub. The sweet aroma of bath salts hung in the air and drifted into other rooms on floors below. The entire house took on a peaceful energy. Daphne checked the temperature of the water and immersed herself. She leaned her head back and gazed through a turret window at a waxing moon.

The enticing lavender-vanilla fragrance conjured memories of earlier years in the Victorian when Daphne fell in love with a ghost. She smiled, recalling how she struggled in fear against the very spirit that ultimately gave powerful meaning to her life. Daphne gently touched her mouth with two fingers to relive her first kiss with Arthur, closed her eyes, and invited a deep sleep. She took her final breath before surrendering into cosmic oneness. Her work on earth was done.

§ § §

Sophia came home two hours later, tired and happy. She called to Daphne, who didn't respond. Sophia tiptoed to Daphne's bedroom suite, but when she smelled the faint, familiar fragrance in the air, she thought not to disturb Daphne's bath. Sophia returned to her own room for the night.

§ § §

The following morning, Sophia found Daphne lying on her bed clothed in a beautiful, cerulean blue satin dress, trimmed with hand-made lace. It hardly seemed possible Daphne was dead, looking gorgeous with rouged cheeks and ruby red lips. Her long hair was neatly combed up with old-fashioned, soft ringlets around her face. She held a small, tightly bound floral bouquet of lavender blossoms—a tussie mussie in a filigree, silver cone.

But Sophia had no doubt—Daphne was gone. The suite emitted a diffused, amber glow she couldn't explain. For an instant, Sophia thought the room had been transformed into a Victorian boudoir with a handsome man in a black waistcoat and matching silk vest. He was standing beside Daphne, looking at his gold pocket watch. When Sophia blinked her eyes, all she could see was Daphne lying there in her usual flannel nightgown.

News traveled fast, and by noon the Victorian's back door was flooded with people bringing food and flowers. Charles arrived just before the ambulance took Daphne's body. He asked to see her one last time. His eyes were red rimmed, and he sat with his head in both hands, distraught. Charles felt guilty for being less available to Daphne after learning how their lives overlapped in different lifetimes. He never told her how uncomfortable it made him and slowly inched away, weary of the supernatural comings and goings that surrounded her. Charles refocused his interests elsewhere, as the city and its anonymity called him again.

§ § §

Daphne's family came as a group the day after Christmas. While waiting for Charles to pick them up at the airport, Nancy and Mary reminisced about their mother. "Mom had an interesting life, but you have to admit, things were a little weird around the house, and it wasn't just the house," Nancy grinned, hoping to cut through Mary's sadness.

They laughed, as did Nancy's husband, Brock, who was carrying Annabelle, sleeping on his shoulder. The child roused. Her excitement about the special gift her grandmother promised preoccupied everyone on the car ride to Franklin Port.

Charles drove onto Main Street. Daphne's daughters braced themselves against their memories. They half expected their mother to be standing on the back porch, greeting them as always. Instead, Sophia met and ushered them to their bedrooms, preserved intact from when they left home many years earlier. It was a somber time for the sisters to be in the dreary house without their mother.

"Oh, Mummy, don't be so sad — we can always talk to Grandma. She's right there," Annabelle said, in her British accent. She led the way back down the staircase as if her grandmother was in the vestibule, waiting to swing her in circles like she remembered on her first visit. "Oh look, Mummy — Grandma is everywhere now, how lovely." Annabelle followed her grandmother to the dining room. "Mummy, I see my present." She called attention to what sat so prettily on the mantle.

Nancy read the gift tag aloud before handing it to Annabelle to open. Untying the ribbon, the girl wanted to wear the jeweled clip right away and asked her mother to pin up her hair the way the lady in the portrait wore hers.

Sophia was mystified, wondering how the portrait changed. She remembered Daphne's chestnut-brown hair painted as flowing over her shoulders. Not wanting to add more complexity to the situation, Sophia decided to let it be, like so many things before.

Annabelle ran into the parlor with the clip in her hair and began dancing and singing to music no one else heard. Daphne's daughters knew the essence of their mother was not lost as Annabelle appeared to be very much like her. Sophia also appreciated the girl filling the emptiness of Daphne's absence so Nancy and Mary could get through the first difficult night in their childhood home.

§ § §

"Amelia, why is Mom having a wake?" Nancy asked as mourners gathered at the funeral home the next day. "It seems out of character for her."

"Sophia said it was your mother's last request. You know, thinking about it, you're right," Amelia said through her tears.

Amelia took a moment to pull Sophia aside. "Are you certain Daphne wanted a wake? She loved hosting parties, but might feel uncomfortable with this display of affection for her."

"Well...I think so." Sophia became confused, hoping she had not misinterpreted Daphne's wishes.

Gwen overheard the conversation. "Do you remember what Daphne told you?"

"She said it would not be such a tragedy to die as long as she had a wake," Sophia struggled to recall.

Gwen chuckled at Sophia's answer. "Did she mean a wake or A. Wake, as in Arthur Wake?" Gwen joked quietly.

Amelia started to giggle, barely containing herself, but held back as people turned to look. "Shh, we'll wake the dead," Amelia sputtered through gushing laughter. "I'll bet Daphne's enjoying this moment. You're off the hook, Sophia. Everything's perfect."

Charles stepped before the people paying their respects. The room hushed. He shared bits of his experiences with Daphne. Everyone smiled over little anecdotes recounting her kookiness. He carefully unfolded a piece of paper to read his final message to her, wherever she was. His voice was somber as he read the words.

Daphne, you changed me like none other,
And I watched you change as well.
Your teachings bring me comfort,
I'll find heaven in my hell.
I'll always love you.

§ § §

The following day, cars lined up behind the hearse. The procession drove through the streets of Franklin Port before climbing the hill to the Hidden Arbor Cemetery.

"I made arrangements for the headstone to be delivered today with a covering. We'll do an unveiling for those who can stay," Nancy told her sister. "We did agree to have her name, dates, and the addition of Forever in Our Hearts, right?"

"Yes, mom would not want anything sappy."

People gathered around the grave. Alex insisted on being first to lay his white rose over Daphne's casket, but as he walked forward, he slipped on an icy patch, landing hard on his right arm. Jason immediately pulled his son to the side, and Sophia and Cassandra hurried after them.

Jason removed the boy's glove and pushed up his coat sleeve to examine the injury. Luckily, it was only a slight bruise. On that sad, overcast day, an eerie glow illuminated Alex's V-shaped birthmark. He self-consciously covered his wrist with the other hand. "Daddy, there's a man standing behind you, staring at me," Alex whispered into his father's ear so his grandmother and mother would not hear.

Jason ushered his family back to the ceremony, but not without turning to see the person his son was talking about. An older man was walking away. He stopped and looked again at Alex and then at the entire family. A shiver ran up Jason's spine.

When it was time for the unveiling, Nancy stepped forward and removed the cloth.

Daphne Lily Betel
1926 – 1956
But Only for an Instant

"Nancy, I thought we agreed to have something else written. What do those words mean? And — look at the date — this is 1974," Mary cried out, devastated.

"1956…1956…wasn't that the year mom had her drowning accident?" Nancy pondered.

"Yes…you're right. What's going on? Did you tell the engraver about her near death by mistake?"

"No, certainly not. Let it go for now. I'll take this up with the engraver later," Nancy said, comforting her sister.

When the funeral was over, friends and family left for Daphne's house. Nancy immediately phoned the man who prepared her mother's headstone. He explained their request was written properly and had no idea how it changed. Because Daphne's daughters were returning to Europe and had much to do before leaving, they put it out of their minds.

No one further pondered the inscription, unaware their perception of reality was being altered. If they revisited the gravesite, they would find the tombstone exactly as Nancy ordered in the first place, but as mortals, they didn't understand what was being orchestrated from the Other Side.

§ § §

Over the next two weeks, Nancy and Mary packed most of Daphne's possessions. They shipped abroad what they wanted to keep while donating or selling the rest. From her guesthouse window, Cassandra watched people carrying items out of the Victorian. She did not know what was to become of the property. Daphne's promise for her and Jason to stay as long as they wanted no longer held. When Cassandra looked over her garden and thought about the business she built, she seethed, realizing everything was coming to an end. Sophia assured Cassandra no formal decisions were made, and Nancy would inform them once the legalities were settled.

§ § §

The anxiously awaited meeting was finally called. Sophia, Cassandra, and Jason sat around the dining table with Daphne's daughters, while Alex played on the floor. The inevitable was announced—the property was going up for sale. Cassandra's heart sank at the loss of her dream.

She turned to the portrait of Daphne and muttered under her breath. In the painting, Daphne's hair was swept up by the diamond studded clip—the same one Cassandra borrowed for her wedding. But like Daphne's daughters, Cassandra wasn't aware the painting changed.

The front doorbell rang, and Nancy invited in the owner of Palmoure Realty who introduced himself as Norman. All these years later, he was still slick. When Mary joined Nancy in the vestibule, he suddenly stood a little taller and smoothed back his thinning hair. "I sold this place eighteen years ago," he bragged, but to no one's interest. "And I'll take care of all the furniture for you," he added, sounding like he was doing the women a favor.

"The furniture is going to auction, Mr. Palmoure," Nancy told him. "I'm expecting the antiques dealer any minute to clear the place out."

Before Norman could say another word, Annabelle came into the room and coaxed Alex into playing a game of hide and seek while Daphne's daughters showed the realtor around the grounds and guesthouse. Cassandra was shattered when she saw Annabelle wearing the hair clip. Tears streamed down her face. Jason pulled his chair closer to comfort her, only now realizing how disrupted his family was about to become.

Alex crawled under the table to see if Annabelle was hiding there. He hit his head and bawled, just as she whisked off. Cassandra bent down to check Alex for a bump, but he darted away with Sophia following him. While pulling herself back up off the floor, Cassandra spotted words burned into the wood on the table's apron.

"Well, look at this—Daphne left a promise to her students. Yeah, sure... this is one promise she can't keep."

"What do you mean by a promise?" Jason asked.

"I promise to foster student dreams, Even if by curious means, And by these words I shall abide," she read.

Cassandra moved away, feeling the promise had no meaning anymore. Jason took a look at the writing himself. "But Cassie, you missed the last part. I am with you from the Other Side."

Cassandra was unimpressed. Convinced everything was being taken away, she watched through the window as the realtor and Nancy entered the guesthouse. What Jason read began to slowly sink in. "Those extra words weren't there before. Something weird is happening."

She read the message a second time. A final sentence had appeared, shaking her out of self-pity. It reminded her of the dried-up well flowing again in the cemetery garden. "Daphne, are you helping us?"

The doorbell rang, sounding more like a wind chime. The antiques dealer and his workers arrived with a huge truck. Mary ran from the guest-house and intercepted them at the back door to supervise the removal of Daphne's furniture. Mary told Cassandra she also made plans for the contents of the guesthouse to go, but not until the property was sold. Cassandra's family could stay on until then.

Saving the dining room furniture for last, the dealer first removed the portrait of a young, Victorian woman with upswept hair held in place by a diamond hair clip. He carefully wrapped it into a clean moving blanket. The men came back inside to load what items were left—the table and chairs.

Jason stopped them. "I'm buying this set."

Cassandra was surprised. "What are you doing? We don't even have a place to live."

"Cassie, we have to begin somewhere. You and I held hands over this table when we were first introduced. This was where it all started for us."

"Yeah, and this is where it's all ending," Cassandra lamented, and then corrected herself. "You might be right. Instead of an end, maybe this is a new beginning."

For the next hour, while the children frolicked and the adults addressed the business at hand, Jason and Cassandra sat quietly on their chairs at the table, the only pieces remaining in the vacant, cavernous house. Once Norman and the others left, Nancy and Mary said their goodbyes and drove away to stay at the Moon Tide Bed and Breakfast until they returned to Europe in a few days. On the way to Amelia and Thad's, they saw a SOLD sign on the lawn of the Port Empress Inn.

As Sophia rounded up Alex, Cassandra could no longer bear more upheaval and stomped out the back, tripping over a package left on the door's threshold. It was wrapped in tattered brown paper, tied with twine. Hand-written across the front was—Jason and Cassandra. She brought it inside and plopped it on the table.

"What's that?" Jason asked. The contents seemed as if they would burst through the wrapping as he untied the familiar bundle and stared in disbelief.

"What is it? What now?" Cassandra edged over to see. She got a glimpse of names embossed on a battered, leather-bound portfolio. "Jason and Cassandra...who...?"

Jason was holding the portfolio he found behind the pivoting panel at the Port Empress Inn years ago, but Dr. Arthur Wake's name on the outside was gone. There was no longer a lock and he opened it easily, dumping the contents across the table while Cassandra sat down, unable to utter a sound. The first thing to fall out was the old, yellowed letter Jason remembered slipping into the portfolio's flap. He read it aloud.

July 4th, 1923

My Dearest Brother Arthur,

My behavior has wronged you beyond words. I am sorry, so very sorry. I loved Olivia, but was too shy to ask her to marry me. I was beside myself on discovering Olivia was marrying you and did everything possible to hurt you both. I went mad, absolutely mad. Father left us a fortune, but I persuaded him to give me complete control of the money. I stole your part of the inheritance. However, it was always my intention to bring you the full amount of your half, as I never spent a penny of it.

You, dear brother, were the golden child and I, much younger and less able, felt like the diminished son in father's eyes. It is not that I wished you less, but that I wished myself more. Upon Olivia's tragic death in my home, I have longed to heal the rift between us. I grew to love AJ dearly, and I understand the deep pain causing you to distance yourself from us both, even though you loved your son more than life itself.

Please do not blame me for the near mishap today at the dock. I saw you running greater than human speed and risking your own life to save your son. It was an act so loving, it brought me to tears. My crew saw AJ fall into the water and already had the schooner under control, but you didn't trust me.

Arthur, I love him as my own. Don't shut me out of his life, I beg you. He's all we have left of our dear Olivia. Can't you find it in your heart to make peace with these circumstances as Olivia wanted?

Simon

Cassandra cried, wondering why the letter wasn't mailed. "Gosh, there's so much power in asking to be forgiven."

Jason didn't respond. He was deep in thought. All the different events he couldn't figure out before were whirling around in his head. He picked up the old picture he found in the pile of woodwork after ripping apart the Port Empress Inn. It was the photograph of a woman standing between two men. For the first time, he turned it over and read what was scrolled across the back, words from Simon that now had meaning. Arthur, Olivia, and me—my heart is broken.

The Wake family saga was beginning to make sense to Jason. So many unspoken feelings and so much unresolved anger among family members were buried with them, brother against brother—ultimately alienating father and son.

Jason handed the letter and picture to Cassandra while he sifted through the pile of envelopes. Some of them had words written in old-fashioned calligraphy—Stocks, Bank Notes, and Deeds. He opened one oversized envelope filled with currency in large denominations. At first glance, the total of everything would appear to be valued in the millions.

"Look," Cassandra cried out, picking up a stack of papers clipped together. "Here is a deed for the Hidden Arbor homestead. What is all this?" Bewildered, Cassandra dove again into the pile of papers, and everything she pulled out had her and Jason's name but...

"Jason, why do all these official papers have our last name as—Wake? Are you a Wake? Am I a Wake?"

Jason couldn't explain. They were holding a fortune in their hands, but who were Jason and Cassandra Wake? At that moment, Sophia entered the dining room carrying Alex, asleep in her arms. She started walking toward the back door.

"Mom...? Where are you going?"

Jason dropped the papers on the table to follow her while Cassandra continued to read through them. As if in a trance, Sophia opened the back door, and on the porch was a robust, well-dressed man in his fifties, smiling at her. Sophia stood there, still lovely—the Goddess from across the lake.

Alex opened his eyes. "Daddy, that's the man I saw staring at me when I fell in the cemetery."

Jason took the boy from Sophia's arms, as he bunched up his shirt to remind his father of the injury. The man outside responded to the child by bunching up his coat sleeve and extending his right arm to show them something.

The stranger's wrist began to glow enough to illuminate a mark on his skin, a V-shaped birthmark—an arrow—exactly as Alex had.

"Just like me, Daddy," Alex shouted, pulling on his father's collar for understanding.

Jason turned to face his mother. "Do you know this man, mom?" he asked her.

The stranger outside stood with complete humility, waiting for either rejection or acceptance. Sophia took her time to find the words. "He's your father, Jason. I remember it all now. I saw the mark on his wrist in the light of a bonfire. He told me it would someday bring him good luck and show the way to his fortune. It's a mark he said always skipped a generation in his family and needed a perfect genetic coupling to reappear. He's your grandfather, Alex."

Sophia spoke through tears of joy as memories from her youth unfolded one after the other. She looked back at the man. "Now I remember you told me you were called AJ."

Upon Sophia's invitation, Arthur Jeffreys Wake stepped into the kitchen of his childhood house. He avoided returning home his entire adult life because he never felt loved by his father. When he received the portfolio years before and read his uncle's letter, he realized how wrong he was and how little he understood his father's pain. With Gwen's note of wise advice, he was able to see his father differently and could finally open his heart for healing to begin.

Deciding to revisit his childhood home and lay hurt to rest once and for all, he contacted Palmoure Realty, who sold it upon his father's death. AJ asked to be apprised if the Victorian ever went back up for sale and was shocked to find out its owner just died. He knew then his father's intricate plan over the years was to show him the way to a greater fortune—his family.

AJ removed a small, silver box from his pocket, kneeled on one knee, and opened it before the woman he never forgot and always dreamed about. Inside was a rare, pink diamond ring.

§ § §

"Don't look back," Dr. Arthur Wake advised his beloved as he pulled her across the firmament. "You are no longer Daphne. It was but only for an instant you thought you were."

Confused, exhilarated, awed, Daphne allowed for the final punctuation of her earthly life. She took her spirit lover's hands and transformed into a light so bright, all physical form dissolved.

"Have we done it, Arthur? Have we helped our son to love?"

"We have done all we could, dear Olivia. It's up to the mortals now."

§ § §

Everyone in the kitchen heard a crash coming from the dining room. The curious placard, Doctor Is In, fell off the massive table and landed face down on the floor.

Season of Mists
by Jennifer Corkill

Justine Holloway prepares for her début into Society, compliments of her godparents, while the under-world of London groans with unfettered abhorrence. When a deadly vampire makes his devious intentions known, her survival might depend on a mysterious Egyptian. Unfortunately, he can't figure out why he's so drawn to her, and whether he must kill her to save humanity.

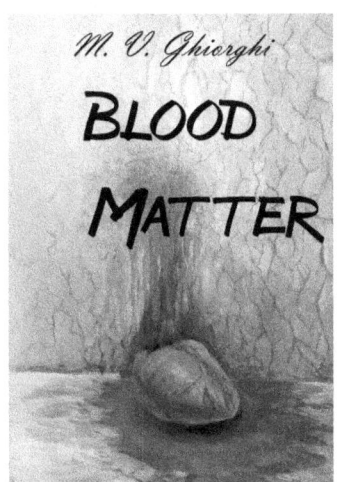

Blood Matters
by M.V. Ghiorghi

A broken-hearted FBI Agent on the run from his demons…a sadistic genius with a penchant for vengeance…a beautiful forensic psychiatrist with a monstrous past…A doomed love triangle born of crime. Can Agent Vasquez survive the *Blood Matter*?